ENCHANTED BY JOJI

A SWEET ROMANTIC COMEDY

REMI CARRINGTON

PHREY PRESS

ISBN-13: 978-1-947685-58-1

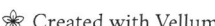 Created with Vellum

CHAPTER 1

JOJI

fter shifting my lifted pickup into park, I engaged the parking brake. The last thing I needed was my brand-new truck rolling away. I scrambled to the ground, then fished the key out of my pocket. The colorful goat key chain I'd purchased was a tad bulky, but it made the key easy to find.

The gate hadn't been closed when I'd visited before, but it was now. I stuck the key into the lock one way, but it wouldn't go in. It didn't help that my hands were shaking with excitement. I inserted the key the opposite way. Success. My new adventure was becoming a reality.

With the gate unlocked, I gave the rusty metal a shove, and it swung open, singing a shrill song as it went. After stuffing the key back into my pocket, I climbed—literally—back into my lifted truck.

I'd traveled the world long enough. It was time to put down roots. But alone and independently wealthy, I needed something to keep me busy, so I bought a goat farm.

Was I crazy for buying it? Probably. I knew absolutely nothing about goats . . . or any other kind of livestock, for that matter. I'd never owned any sort of a pet. Not even a goldfish.

Checking my mirrors to make sure I cleared the gate on both sides, I drove my brand-new pickup through the gate.

Clint Jackson, the guy who was going to teach me all I needed to know about goat farming, wasn't supposed to meet me for another twenty minutes. That gave me time to look around again. I'd been here twice before and toured the place, but it somehow looked different now that it was mine.

That sounded silly. But it was true. Everything I could see was now mine.

The stone house was simple but spacious. Plenty big for one person. And the big front porch opened its arms in welcome. Detached from the house, the garage was large enough to house my classic Mustang, but not sized to hold my purple goddess. A few hundred feet from the house was a trailer home. I'd have to ask about that.

My main interest at the moment was the barn. It was huge. I couldn't imagine filling it with goats. Or maybe the goats preferred living outside.

I had lots of questions. Luckily, someone was coming to answer them.

When I'd purchased the goat farm from Mr. Henry who owned the adjoining ranch, he offered for his ranch foreman to teach me what I needed to know to run the place. Free help wasn't an offer I was going to turn down. That would save me hours of Googling.

I parked my purple goddess—because a truck like this needed a fabulous name—in front of the house, then swung open the door. The side step unfolded, making it possible to get out. Possible was not the same as easy. Gripping the steering wheel, I lowered myself to the step. Once there I sat down and dangled my feet off the side.

Why had I purchased a lifted truck? The roads back here

on the ranch didn't require such a high lift, but I was a bit infatuated with my new toy.

As soon as my feet hit the ground, I took off in search of the goats. Mr. Henry had mentioned that most had been sold, but there were a few still around. I could acquire more goats once I got the hang of things.

Those furry little creatures weren't hard to find. One was making a huge ruckus, so I followed the noise.

In the barn, I peeked into a stall, and two little baby goats shouted at me. What was the noise a goat makes called? I knew the word. Why couldn't I think of it?

"Hey there. You must be hungry. I'll see what I can find for you. But Mr. Clint should be here soon, and he knows all about goats. Give me a second. I need to check and see who is making all the noise."

I walked through the barn, peeking into each stall as I went. Just out the back door, I found the crier in the pen attached to the barn. From the looks of the goat, it was a mama. And she was ready to feed someone.

It was a good thing I'd shown up early. Those babies were hungry.

Who had put them in separate pens? That didn't make any sense at all.

I ran back into the barn, swung open the stall door and patted my leg. Like well-trained dogs, the kids ran up to me, then followed me out of the barn.

Mama goat ran to the fence, clearly excited.

The gate took a second to figure out, but I managed. I stepped away to grab the babies who were running along the fence next to the mama goat. Catching them was difficult, and holding onto them was equally hard. They wriggled a lot. With an arm around each one, I turned just in time to see one of the other goats run out of the gate. She or he—I couldn't tell without investigating—didn't wander far, so I saw no harm in allowing a few minutes of freedom.

The babies ran to their mama, and I walked over to the other pen. One goat was standing on its hind legs eating leaves off a tree. Laughing, I watched the antics. After a minute, I caught motion on one of the higher branches.

How had a goat gotten up there? He must be stuck.

I let myself in the gate, found a barrel, and rolled it toward the tree. After shoving on it to make sure it felt strong enough to hold me, I climbed onto it, then jumped to catch hold of the tree limb. Graceful did not describe my climbing skills. It was a good thing no one was around to see this.

The goat bleated at me. That was the word I couldn't think of earlier. Bleated.

"I'm coming. How in the world did you get up so high?" Dangling from the limb, I inhaled before swinging my leg up. The first attempt didn't end in success. But the second attempt was better. With one leg on the lowest limb, I scooched my body up. It took a bit of work, but once I was on the branch, I shifted toward the trunk and looked up.

The goat was another two limbs up.

I could do this.

With my arms wrapped around the trunk, I shinnied up even with the goat.

"I'm almost to you." I wriggled my way out onto the limb. "Come over here, and I'll help you down."

That creature looked at me like I was made of bubbles. He hopped from one branch to another, and in no time, that goat was on the ground and running for the gate I'd failed to close.

I had a feeling Clint was not going to be pleased.

But that was the least of my worries. I was up in the stupid tree.

Working my way backward, I stopped when the branch creaked. I was a long way from the ground. But I couldn't stay up in the tree. Moving slowly, I inched back. When I reached the trunk, I shinnied down to the limb below me.

After a short pause to get my bearings, I started down again. Just as I made it far enough down the tree to drop onto the barrel without killing myself, those blasted goats knocked it over.

"Hey! Put that back." As if I had any chance of changing their minds by hollering at them. "I won't forget this!"

Besides, it wasn't like they could get the barrel upright again.

I hadn't even counted to know how many goats I'd just let loose.

Without the barrel, there was no way I was getting out of this tree without turning an ankle or breaking a leg. I needed help.

Had it been twenty minutes yet?

I'd managed alone so far in life, and since I planned to run this place by myself, I needed to start acting like it now. I wrapped my arms around the large tree limb, interlocking my fingers on the top side. Then I let one leg slide off the branch. The other leg followed even though I wasn't quite ready.

My arms scraped against the bark, and my fingers started to slip apart. This wasn't good.

Hanging from the tree like a monkey, I focused on keeping my hands joined. Not falling was my goal. Forget trying to do everything on my own. I needed help.

A door slammed, and I hoped it was Clint . . . or anyone tall enough to get me out of the tree. Looking back over my shoulder, I spotted the goats ratting me out. They ran up to him, bragging about how they were out of their pens.

Barrel-chested, the man towered over me by about fifteen

inches. That was a guess since I'd only met him once. But I'd paid attention.

He had a boyish face, but that was the only boyish thing about him. The rest of him was all man. Big, strong man.

Why was I thinking about that now? But gosh, those fifteen inches were going to come in handy.

Just shy of fifty, I wasn't in the market for a special someone. However, I could see. And Clint was pleasant on the eyes. It was easier to think about him than my predicament.

He rubbed the back of his neck. "How'd y'all get out? Never mind. I don't think I want to know." He glanced around. "Mrs. Sparks?"

"It's *Miss* Sparks. There isn't and never was a Mr. Sparks. I mean, my dad was Mr. Sparks, but, you know what, just call me Joji. That's short for Georgia Jean. My mama called me that when I found trouble, or more often, when trouble found me." Why was I saying all this? I should've been shouting for him to get me down.

He broke into a run. "Why are you in the tree?" His paced slowed as he entered the fenced area. "You goats, back in the pen."

They obeyed.

Then he closed the gate. I'd have to remember that trick.

I smiled as he sauntered toward me. "I climbed up here to help a goat down. Turned out, he didn't need my help, but then the fool goats knocked over the barrel."

One side of his mouth lifted ever so slightly. "Well, Georgia Jean, seems to me you found trouble."

"Are you going to laugh at me or help me down?"

"Both. Are you about to fall?"

"Who said anything about falling? I'm just hanging around." It was hard to act indignant dangling from a tree limb.

"Aren't you a funny one?" He stepped right below me.

"Didn't I say that if you arrived before I got here to just wait for me?" His tone was a little condescending.

"I am waiting. Is waiting up in a tree so strange?"

"Yes." He grabbed my boots, then slid his hands up over his head until he had me just below the hips. Looking up, he stared at me. "All right, Trouble, this is what you're going to do. Let go of that branch, and I'll catch you." He widened his stance.

"Did you just call me Trouble?"

He nodded. "If you can ease down, I'll work you toward the ground."

"Here goes." I pried my fingers apart, hoping to keep hold of the branch and lower myself until he had a good hold. But as soon as my hands disconnected, my arms slid across the bark, and I plummeted.

He grabbed my legs.

I braced my hands on his shoulders, and slowly, he shifted me closer to the ground.

Did I mention his chest? If I hadn't noticed it before, having my entire body slide down the front of him made that broad, manly chest very noticeable.

If I were feeling extra mischievous one day, I'd climb the tree again, just to have him help me down a second time. But first I needed to give the scratches on my arms time to heal.

Just before my face collided with his hat, I lifted it off his head.

His head jerked up, and I stopped sliding. Face to face, we stared at each other.

This was not how I expected my adventure to start.

"I've held kittens that weighed more than you do." He glanced at his hat in my hand. "Be careful with my hat."

"You holding a kitten. That is something I want to see."

He turned when a goat bleated. "You let Lucy out."

"Maybe." I shrugged. "Which one is Lucy?"

Clint motioned to a goat that had another goat behind it, and he—I had no doubts about that one being a guy—um, looked happy to see Lucy.

"Looks like you might have new goats in about five months. Not exactly what I planned." Still holding me, Clint shook his head.

"Is that a problem?"

"I hope not. That's his sister."

"Sorry, she got out when I was letting the baby goats into the pen with their mama."

He shook his head. "If these two kids quit taking the bottle, I swear . . ."

"The bottle? But their mama . . ."

"For a small thing, you sure make a mess." He didn't seem like he was in a hurry to put me down.

Was this his quiet show of force, trying to show me who was in charge?

If he wanted to play games, I could have fun with this. I leaned closer until my nose almost touched his. "We aren't going to get much done if you keep holding me like this."

He put me down faster than shooting stars streak across the night sky. "Stay out of the tree."

"I can't promise anything." I dusted off my jeans.

"*Please* stay out of the tree." He was a quick learner.

"Okay." I made sure he didn't see my fingers crossed under his hat as I handed it back.

"I've got to get those kids back into their own pen." He marched away.

I watched the label on his jeans a second before chasing after him. Having him around would be quite fun.

CHAPTER 2

CLINT

I'd spent over an hour last night trying to convince Beau to send someone else to teach Miss Sparks about goat farming. Beau was my boss, but we'd been friends since before high school. He knew the two reasons I didn't want anything to do with this job. I hated goats. And I had an only slightly milder dislike of redheads.

And this Georgia Jean had hair as red as the stripes on Old Glory.

Why hadn't I become a banker or a doctor?

Joji ran to catch up with me and looped her arm around mine. "Where do we start?"

Without trying to be subtle, I yanked my arm away. "You can watch me milk the mama goat."

"Does she have a name?"

"Does it matter? They're goats."

"Even goats deserve to be called by name." This woman said the oddest things.

I pulled open the barn door and motioned for Joji to go in. "Ladies first."

"Ooh, manners. How fun!" She wasn't going to make any of this easy.

Growing up, my family raised goats. I'd lived and breathed goat farming for years, and when I left home, I vowed never to be around goats again. A lot of good that did me.

I pointed to the stand set up near one wall of the barn. "That's the milking station. I'll show you all the things you need to have ready before you start milking."

"Should I write this down?" She rubbed at scratches on her arms.

"Need something for those?" I felt bad that she'd ended up hurt.

Her red curls danced when she shook her head. "Nah, I'll be fine."

"Don't worry about writing anything down. Just watch." If I could keep her focused on one thing at a time, we'd get through this training before my sanity flew the coop.

I prepped the milking station, showing her everything she needed to complete the task. And it took longer than normal because the woman questioned everything.

She ran a finger along the top of the pail. "Does it matter if it's a metal bucket?"

"No."

"Did I mess up the milking by letting the babies get to their mama?" She cocked her head to one side and looked up at me.

"Yes." I sat down on the milking stool.

"Sorry." She crinkled her nose. "How long does the mama cry?"

I rubbed the back of my neck, reminding myself to be nice. "Can we please focus on the milking?"

"I'm just trying to learn." She hovered right beside me. "Do the goats prefer to sleep outside or inside? How long does the mama goat produce milk after the babies are born? Why do you separate the babies from the mama?"

I turned and ended up nose to nose with her again. When she smiled, I shifted away. "They are milking goats. If the babies stay with the mama, guess who gets the milk."

"So what do you feed the babies?"

"We give them milk from the mama, but her production is higher if we milk her and feed the babies from that."

She inched closer again. "Makes sense. Then more milk for me to make cheese."

I shouldn't have asked, but my curiosity got the better of me. "You make cheese?"

"I took a class. I haven't made any on my own yet, but there's a first time for everything." She clapped her hands together. "Are we finally ready to do the milking?"

"Wait here. I'll get Maude."

Joji popped her hands on her hips. "You do know her name."

"I know all their names."

She grabbed my arm. "Before the end of today's lesson, I want you to teach me all the names."

What was with all the touching?

"Sure." The sooner I ran through the morning chores, the sooner I could head back to the ranch and put distance between me and the touching.

As soon as I opened the gate, Maude ran toward the platform. She knew what was waiting in the feed trough.

Joji's eyes were wide with excitement. "She likes being milked?"

"She likes what's in the trough. Once she's in place, you adjust this and lock it so she can't pull out."

She slapped a hand over her heart. "It's like a torture device!"

"It is not hurting her at all. It keeps her from running off. Have you ever tried to milk a goat that's on the move?"

Joji tilted her head back, and laughter bubbled out of her. "I can almost picture you chasing after her, trying to hang on."

"I'm glad you're entertained."

She patted my shoulder. "You're cute."

Dealing with goats was easier than being around my redheaded student.

Ignoring her last comment, I continued with the lesson. "First, you want to wipe down her udder. Then the first squirts get discarded, so use this other pan for that."

She nodded.

"Then you put the pail under her and start milking." I demonstrated how to do it.

Joji rested a hand on my back and leaned in so close I wasn't sure if it was her breathing or mine that I was hearing.

"So you're just pulling on it."

"No, I'm squeezing here at the top." There wasn't much in Maude after she'd fed the two little ones, so milking her didn't take long. I wiped her down again, then led her back to her pen. "Soon, you'll be doing the milking, and I'll watch."

Joji danced a little jig. "I'm so excited. I can't believe this is going to be my life."

"I can't imagine why anyone would choose this life." I picked up the milk. "Normally, I'd feed the babies next, but that's already been taken care of. Let's go filter the milk and get it in the fridge."

"I left the keys to the house in my truck." Joji ran her fingers through her curls, leaving red hairs pointing in a hundred different directions.

I jingled the keys dangling off my belt loop. "I've got it."

"I'm not sure how I feel about you having keys to my place. We don't even know each other that well."

If she kept making comments like that, I'd probably go crazy before she knew how to run the farm.

I slid the key off my ring. "Here."

She shook her head. "You keep it. Just in case."

Tonight, I'd spend another hour trying to convince Beau to let me out of the job. I could teach one of the other ranch hands how to take care of goats. It wasn't rocket science.

AFTER TWO HOURS teaching Joji the morning routine, I walked toward my truck. "I'll be back this evening, and we'll go through the evening routine."

She stepped in front of me. "Before you go, will you help me with something?"

"Depends." I knew better than to commit to something before getting details.

"I like you. You say what you think."

We had that in common. She just said more of what she thought.

I inched back from her. "What do you need?"

"There are two suitcases in the back of my truck. Would you, pretty please, help me take them inside?"

"I can do that. When does the moving truck arrive?"

"Tomorrow. About noon, I think."

I lifted two extremely heavy suitcases out of the bed of the truck. "Where are you sleeping tonight?"

"I have a sleeping bag."

"After we finish tonight, I'll drive you to Ava's. My sister won't care if you stay at her place."

Joji didn't look like the sleeping-on-the-floor type.

"Older or younger? Are you the big brother or the baby brother?" She stood looking up at me, squinting one eye. "Don't tell me. Let me guess."

I shifted around her and carried the bags into the house.

"That was a big-brother move. And you don't seem like a baby at all." She walked down the hall. "Just bring those back to my bedroom."

I set the bags in the corner of her room. "I'll be back later."

"You don't like me, do you?" She stood in the doorway, blocking my escape.

"I have no issue with you." I moved to step around her.

She shifted to stop me. "Is it because I talk a lot?"

"You can talk all you want."

"I wasn't asking if I should talk less. I asked if that was why you didn't like me."

She gasped as I gripped her waist, lifted her off the ground, and moved her out of my way.

"Never said I didn't like you." I strode down the hall.

Running to keep up, she said, "I'm not great at interpreting grunts, but I've gotten that impression."

Giving her part of the truth would hopefully end this conversation. "I don't like goats."

She followed me out to the porch. "How can you not like goats?"

"I'm heartless that way." I tipped my hat. "See ya later."

Arms folded across her chest, she leaned on the doorframe. "I eagerly await your return."

I slammed the door of my truck as she laughed. It was going to be a long couple of weeks.

CHAPTER 3

Standing in the barn, I laid out the assortment of items Clint had used for milking. I wanted to memorize what was needed. Because when he showed up for tonight's lesson, I intended to demonstrate what a quick learner I was.

With everything sitting out, I ran through the routine in my head, making sure I hadn't missed anything. Dang it. I'd forgotten the rag. The cleaning solution wouldn't do me much good without something I could use to wipe down the udder.

Until it all became second nature, I needed something to help me remember. Touching the items one at a time, I made up a rhyme.

Once I was sure I could prep for milking without Clint telling me what to grab, I wandered out to the pen where the baby goats romped.

Inside the gate, I sat down on the ground. "Y'all sure are cute." I scratched them as they climbed in and out of my lap.

It had been a long time since I'd done yoga, but I wanted

to know how these little ones would react. I'd heard of places that hosted goat yoga classes, and I wanted to offer that here.

There was a whole list of basic poses, but I could only remember two. I stood and touched my hands together above my head, then balanced on one foot. As soon as I was in position, one of those little cuties ran headfirst into my leg.

"Hey there. That's no way to behave." I caught myself before hitting the ground. People would definitely have to sign waivers.

After loving on both little goats, I stretched into the downward dog position. We'd need mats because no one but me would be silly enough to put their head on the ground.

To the goats, I looked like a ramp. Bleating, they jumped on my back. One ran off right away but the other balanced on my butt, which was sticking up in the air.

Laughing, I shoved away the kid chewing on my hair. "No, sir. Don't eat my hair."

"What in the world are you doing?"

When had Clint returned?

I tried to shoo the goat off my butt so I could stand up. "Go on, now. I need to get up."

"Just get up. He'll figure it out." Clint hovered next to me. "He's a goat."

"I know." I stood and pulled grass out of my hair. "Goat yoga."

"Goat what?" He crinkled his nose. "Did you hit your head?"

"No. I was seeing how these guys would do if I hosted a goat yoga class."

He laughed. Not a small, polite chuckle. "Are *you* going to teach it?"

"Are you laughing at me?"

One of the baby goats ran around Clint's feet, begging for attention. Why did the little ones even bother?

"Sure am. Ava sent me to invite you to lunch. She made chili and cornbread." He picked up the goat and scratched the top of its head.

I couldn't figure this guy out. For someone who hated goats, he wasn't acting like it.

I dusted off my jeans. Again. "And here I thought you'd just come back to see me."

"Are you disappointed?" He set the goat down and petted the other before shoving his hands in his pockets.

"Lunch sounds great."

"Hop in." He strode back toward his truck.

His long stride made it hard to keep up with him, and I almost had to run.

He opened the door for me. In spite of his gruff exterior, chivalry and manners were part of who he was. That was already obvious. It was the less-obvious stuff that had me curious.

Getting into his truck was easier than climbing into mine. "I memorized everything needed for milking."

"Good. You can pull it all out tonight." The truck kicked up dust as he pulled away from the barn.

"Where are you going? The main gate is that way."

"Don't trust me?"

"What's with the questions as answers?"

"Does that bother you?" His quick wit was attractive.

"No, actually, I find you very engaging." I hadn't known him long, but I was figuring out how to get certain reactions.

"I'm headed to the back gate. Takes us to the ranch."

Flirting almost always garnered me straight and simple answers. "You don't even have to get on roads to come see me."

He turned up the radio.

I was going to enjoy learning from Clint. It was possible I'd drive him crazy, but it wasn't my intent. I just wanted to know what was beneath that crusty exterior.

When he parked, I jumped out before he had a chance to show off his manners. Young men in dusty jeans and well-worn boots filed into what I assumed was a dining room. It was an addition to a rather large house.

"Is that where we eat?" Taking out my phone and snapping pictures would be too obvious, but some of these guys would make great posters.

Clint took off toward the house. "That's the mess hall."

"And who are all those guys?" I grabbed his arm, hoping he'd slow his pace a little.

"Ranch hands."

"I wonder if they'd be willing to do goat yoga. I bet women would pay money to watch that."

He stopped and stared at my hand on his arm. "You're nuttier than a fruitcake."

If it weren't for the amusement dancing in his eyes, I might've been offended. "I've never had fruitcake. Do they put nuts in them?" What I really wanted to know was if Clint liked fruitcake.

Rolling his eyes, he started walking again. "Go on in. I have stuff to do." He veered around the house and disappeared.

I was starting to get the distinct impression that Clint's assertion that he hadn't said he didn't like me was a technicality. He hadn't said it, but based on all the clues, he didn't like me much.

I'd have to try harder to win him over.

When I stepped inside, Ava met me at the door. "Come in. I figured Clint would be with you."

"I think I scared him off."

She laughed. "Makes sense. Food is over there. Help yourself. Then I'll introduce you to everyone."

"Clint offered for me to stay in your guest room tonight since my furniture doesn't arrive until tomorrow. Is that all right with you?"

"Of course! You're always welcome. I'll make us a chocolate cake. And I'll see if Lilith wants to join us . . . if she can drag herself away from Beau."

I sorted through names in my head. "Beau is the owner, and Lilith is his wife?"

"That's right." Ava motioned toward the counter. "I'll save you a seat."

I washed my hands, then filled a bowl with food. Learning about the farm and playing with goats had given me quite an appetite.

When I dropped into the chair beside Ava, she set her fork down. "Boys, this is Joji. She's the new owner of the goat farm."

Polite nods and greetings echoed from around the table.

A figure appeared in the doorway, and I didn't need to look up to know who it was.

"Thanks, everyone. I'm in way over my head, but Clint is teaching me. It shouldn't take more than a year or two for me to get the hang of things." My comment earned me a few laughs, and one snort.

Clint stomped to the counter and picked up a bowl.

Ava patted my arm. "Don't take it personally. He's just not excited about teaching you."

"I already figured that out."

He sat at the opposite end of the table and asked the ranch hands about chores and other things that needed to be done around the ranch.

"Is he in charge?" I kept my voice low so I wouldn't interrupt his conversation.

Ava nodded. "Clint is the ranch foreman, but Beau is handling a lot of that right now."

"Because Clint is helping me." I felt a little bad for giving the man a hard time.

"Yep, and tonight I'll tell you all about why it's Clint over there helping and not one of these other guys."

Now I was really curious. "I assumed he was the only one who knew about goats."

"Learning about goats is easy. Any of these guys could've learned in a week." She grinned. "But I don't want to talk about it here."

"Talk about what, Ava?" Clint eyed her from the other end of the table.

I broke off a corner of my cornbread. "Are you going to help me teach the goat yoga classes, Mr. Jackson?"

The ranch hands snickered but didn't look up.

Clint's eye narrowed. "Just say when."

My stomach knotted, and I had the awful feeling that I'd just poked at a beehive. But I wasn't about to show any sign of that in front of all the guys. "I can't wait to see you in those tight little pants."

Ava howled. "All right, you two, take your flirting some-where else. I don't want trouble in here."

Everyone around the table—except Clint and I—started laughing. His gaze dropped to his bowl, and he ignored the others.

I'd definitely stirred up the bees.

CHAPTER 4

CLINT

Silent, I drove Joji back to her place.

"Are you upset with me?" She pursed her lips and raised her eyebrows.

"Nope."

"Really? Because the silent treatment says otherwise." She turned to look out the window.

"Just don't have anything to say." Everything I said ended up twisted and used against me. "House or barn?"

"Doesn't matter."

I stopped halfway between the two. "I'll be back at five."

She slid out of my truck and walked toward the house without turning around. I appreciated her spunk. There weren't many women who would buy a goat farm without knowing anything about how to run it. I just wasn't sure why she'd done it.

I waited until she walked inside before turning the truck around. Then I drove out to meet Beau.

He grinned as I stepped out of the truck. "How are the lessons going?"

"Shut up." I grabbed the roll of barbed wire out of the bed of the truck.

"New post is already in. I finished that while you chauffeured Joji around." He wasn't letting up.

I yanked on my leather gloves. "Want me to roll this out or what?"

He pointed at the fence post. "You do this. I'll roll it out." Holding the bundle of wire, he looked back over his shoulder. "Is it really that bad?"

"Where's the wire stretcher?"

"In my truck."

I grabbed the tool and continued working on the fence. "She's smart. I think she'll catch on quickly."

"From you, that's a downright glowing review."

I shrugged. The woman wasn't dumb. She was just . . . hard not to think about. Especially when Beau kept bringing her up.

But I wasn't about to say that. "She has this idea about hosting goat yoga classes."

"I'll tell Lilith. She might like that." Beau grinned.

"And she wants me to help teach the classes." I knew how to keep the conversation light.

He howled. "Let me know when. I'll be there with bells on."

"Careful what you say. I might hold you to that."

"If you wear those stretchy pants, wearing bells to cheer you on is the least I can do."

"Thanks for that."

We worked in silence for a while.

As I made sure the wire was tight, Beau gathered the tools. "She seems nice."

"Look, I'm doing as you asked, and I'm teaching her how to run the place. You don't pay me enough to talk about it."

"I thought we were friends."

"We are. That's why I haven't punched you." I checked the time. "Gotta go. I told her I'd be there at five."

He yanked off his gloves. "See you at dinner."

I drove back to Joji's, ready to put her memory to the test.

Blaring music greeted me when I arrived at the barn. I hadn't even opened my door, and the place sounded like someone was hosting a rave.

Joji was probably trying to teach the goats to dance.

I hopped out and walked up to the door. With "You Shook Me All Night Long" blasting from a small speaker, Joji danced like no one was watching. But that wasn't the case.

I leaned against the door and waited for the song to end. But when Lynyrd Skynyrd started singing "Sweet Home Alabama," I stayed put and kept quiet. The woman had good taste in music.

She continued to dance. And the baby goats loved it. They ran around her feet, enthralled with the whole scene.

As the song wound to a close, I clapped.

Joji brushed curls out of her face. "Didn't know I had an audience."

"Clearly."

She picked up her phone and turned down the volume. "Are we starting with milking? I can get out all the stuff."

"Yep. Have at it."

Fanning herself, she walked toward the house. "Good thing you clapped. I was considering taking off my shirt."

"I'll remember never to sneak up on you."

"Smart man." She glanced back over her shoulder and winked.

Helping her was more entertaining than I'd admit to anyone.

Inside, as she mixed the cleaning solution and gathered items, her lips moved.

I hovered near the door and couldn't make out what she was saying to herself. So far, she hadn't forgotten anything.

Back in the barn, she set everything on the milking station, then gathered the other things we needed. Once everything was sitting out, she scanned them, touching each item as she sang out a rhyme. "Soap and bucket, milking pail. Feed the goats and feed them well. Lock 'em in and wash 'em down. Now it's time to go to town." She moved down the line. "Waste a squirt, then fill the pail. Dip the teats and clean up well. Fill the jar and take it in. Celebrate another win."

I didn't bother biting back my chuckle. "What are you saying?"

"I made up a rhyme to help me remember everything." She sang it again. "And it worked . . . I think."

"What's that about a win?"

"I needed a line at the end, so I made something up." She pointed at the milking stand. "Do I have everything?"

"Except the goat."

She ran out of the barn. "Hey, Maude. You ready to get a treat?" Her enthusiasm bewildered me. Lots of things about her bewildered me.

Happy to be out of the pen, Maude strolled onto the stand and started eating.

Joji locked the goat into place and wiped down the udder.

"Should I milk her?" Joji perched on the edge of the stand.

"Sure." I leaned over to make sure she had the right hold.

She moved her fingers, but nothing came out.

"Are you squeezing near the top?"

"I am. See?" She pointed the teat right at me and then mastered the art of squeezing.

Milk landed on the front of my jeans. Right on my zipper.

Reaching out, she acted like she was going to wipe it off, but I was quicker than her hand.

"I'm so sorry." Horror swirled in her brown eyes.

"Just milk her. Seems you've figured out how to do it." I grabbed a rag and cleaned my jeans off as best I could.

Joji's shoulders slumped as she went back to milking Maude, and I missed the enthusiasm of the woman who was dancing in the barn just a bit ago.

I squatted beside her, watching as she worked. "That was a well-placed mistake. I'm wondering if you planned that."

She shook her head. "I didn't."

That wasn't the snarky answer I'd expected.

"You're a quick learner. I'm impressed that you remembered everything."

"Don't patronize me." She set her jaw.

"Where I grew up, we call that complimenting someone." I really was trying to be nice.

Her hands continued the alternating motion. "I wanted to prove to you that I could do this right. Next time, I'll be better at it."

"Next time, don't point it at me."

"Or maybe at your face." She looked up at me. "Thanks for suggesting I stay with Ava. I think I'll enjoy getting to know her."

I'd probably regret them becoming friends. "I'm sure y'all will have lots in common."

"Right now, the only thing we have in common is you. I'm sure we'll have lots to talk about." Her smile returned.

"Have fun with that. I'm a pretty boring person."

She moved the bucket to the side, cleaned up Maude, and released the goat from the stand. "Now we feed the babies?"

"I'll walk her back and feed the goats outside. You pour the milk into the jar, then I'll show you how to feed the babies." I led Maude back to her pen.

Joji sang as she poured the milk and cleaned the stand.

In all my years working around animals, I'd never met anyone who sang while they worked. And in her designer jeans and fitted t-shirt, she looked completely out of place in a barn.

I, on the other hand, looked like I'd been raised in one. I just about had been.

CHAPTER 5

*A*va leaned forward, watching as I popped the first bite of chocolate cake into my mouth.

"Good, isn't it?" Lilith danced her fork in the air, using it to accent her words.

"Amazing." I savored the bite, then licked my lips. No sense wasting chocolate. "So, are y'all going to tell me why Clint can't stand me?"

Lilith laughed. "You haven't told her?"

Ava shrugged. "Go ahead."

"Clint hates redheads. Try not to take it personally." Lilith patted my arm. "He's got issues."

"Care to elaborate?" I turned to Ava.

She kept her gaze on her cake. "There's a reason he hates them, but that's his story to tell. I will only say that a redhead up and left him years ago. But he never said why. And there is more to it than just your hair. Clint also doesn't like goats."

"Then why is he out there helping me? Couldn't one of those young, strapping ranch hands give me a lesson or two?"

Laughter echoed off the walls.

"I like you." Lilith licked her fork.

Ava caught her breath, then giggled again. "Beau and Clint have been friends for years. I barely remember a time when they didn't hang out together. So, Beau knows Clint. Knows what he likes and doesn't like." She sipped her red wine. "Need a refill?"

"No. I need you to finish telling me why Clint hates me."

"Anyway, when Beau met Lilith, Clint sort of gave them a hard time. Just a little."

"Because that's what friends do." I could imagine those two guys exchanging verbal jabs.

"Right."

"So, I'm payback." I ate the last bit of my cake, trying to decide what to do with my new bit of knowledge.

Lilith clapped. "Exactly. He's more irritated with Beau than he is frustrated with you."

"I'm not sure that's true. Did he tell you how I squirted him when I was learning to milk Maude?"

"No!" Ava slapped a hand to her mouth.

"Right below the belt." I refilled my wine glass. "I'll be surprised if he even shows up tomorrow."

"He will." Lilith served herself another piece of cake. "He's too ornery to back out."

"That's true." Ava nodded. "I love the man because he's my brother, but he is as stubborn as they come."

My picture of Clint had changed a little. My grumpy cowboy was protecting a broken heart with that crusty exterior.

"Enough about Clint. Tell us about you." Ava hugged a throw pillow to her chest. "Anyone special in your life?"

"Not for many years." Wine rippled across the top of my glass. "I fell in love when I was eighteen. He proposed when I was nineteen, but I didn't answer right away. He didn't have a steady job, a career-type job, and I was afraid people would think he was lazy and couldn't take care of me. My head thought one thing, and my heart wanted something completely different."

"So what happened?" Lilith glanced at her phone.

"He took an odd job helping Old Man Miller repair a dilapidated barn. While up on the roof, Oscar slipped. It happened on my birthday. I never got a chance to tell him I wanted to marry him."

"That's so sad!" Ava wiped her eyes.

"He used to tinker in his garage. That's what he did instead of working a regular day job. What I didn't know was that he'd filed patents on the things he created. And they've earned lots of money over the years. Oscar left everything to me. He's taken care of me all these years. Financially, at least. For the most part, I take care of myself. Life is simpler that way."

Lilith tapped on her phone screen. "Sorry. Beau can't find anything when I'm not around."

Ava shook her head. "Not true. He just plays dumb so she'll help him. Beau took care of himself quite well for years."

"I'm letting him get away with it *for now*." Lilith grinned.

"What about you, Ava?" I debated about whether to have a second slice of cake.

"What about me . . . what?"

"Is there a man in your life?"

"No special someone. I'm content living here and feeding these cowboys. Someone has to do it."

Lilith set her plate aside. "Ava is like a mom to all those guys. This ranch wouldn't be the same without her."

I served myself another piece of cake and listened as Lilith and Ava told stories about the ranch. One person was notably missing from most of the stories—Clint. If I was going to learn more about him, I wasn't going to do it here.

～

CLINT SHOWED up to Ava's incredibly early. I'd only managed to pry one eye open, but I was dressed.

"You ready?"

I nodded and followed him to the truck.

And like yesterday, he put his chivalry on display by opening my door and helping me in.

On the way to the farm, he was quiet. The radio wasn't even playing. I wasn't always chatty before coffee, but this dead silence made me clammy.

I asked a question I hoped would spark conversation. "Did you talk to Beau last night?"

"About?"

"Getting someone else to teach me."

I wasn't quite able to interpret his grunt.

When he parked, I jumped out and gathered what was needed for milking. The sooner we finished the chores, the sooner he could leave. And he clearly didn't want to be here.

After milking Maude and taking the milk inside, I filled up two bottles while Clint fed the big goats.

He dusted off his hands as he walked toward me. "Now we feed the babies. Do you remember what I showed you last night? And did I mention that if you hold them in your lap, they might pee on you."

"Thanks for the warning."

He dropped onto a bench, then set a kid in front of him. "You might have to sort of force it in at first because it takes a little bit for them to get used to the nipple."

"Can I feed the other one?"

"Sure."

I hugged the kid, trying to keep it still while holding the bottle in its mouth. The little one latched on right away and made quick work of the milk.

There was something very satisfying about taking care of the baby goats. After all those years on my own—years when most people were having families—it was nice to have these guys to take care of.

"What's next?"

"That's enough for right now. You've got the moving truck coming, so you'll have plenty to do."

"I paid for an extra moving guy. I'm hoping they are up to the task." If I needed extra help, perhaps I could pay a couple of ranch hands for a few hours work.

"I'll send a couple of guys over." He stopped beside his truck. "Are you going to hang out here? Or do you want a ride to the ranch?"

"Not much I can do here." I climbed into the passenger seat. "Besides, you showed up so early, I forgot my stuff at Ava's."

"Everything around here starts early."

"I'm learning that."

When we got to the ranch, he stopped in front of the main house. "Is your bag packed? If so, I'll grab it."

"It was early. I have no idea if it's packed."

He sighed and turned toward Ava's. "Be quick. I'd like to get a few chores done before I have to take you back." Acting like I was a bother irritated me.

"Don't worry about me. I'll find a ride. They have Uber and Lyft around here, don't they?"

He chuckled and stopped in front of Ava's. "I'll wait here."

"I wonder if it's locked."

"No one locks doors around here."

I glanced at the other house a few hundred yards away. "Is that your place?"

He turned on the radio, which I took to mean yes.

Biting back a laugh, I slid out and ran inside.

It only took a few minutes to shove my things into the bag. Then I ran back out to the truck. "Did you time me?"

"Five minutes twenty-two seconds." He pulled away from the house. "I'll drop you at the main house. I'll be back at eleven-thirty to run you back. If you need me sooner, have Ava text me."

"I have your number."

He shrugged.

Before getting out at the main house, I turned to face him. "Eventually, I'll figure out how to get you to stop hating me."

"I don't hate you."

"Hello?" I tugged on one of my curls. "I like to call it copper, but to you, it apparently looks red."

He rolled his head from side to side. "They told you."

"Ding, ding, ding! We have a winner." I jumped out and waved.

He drove away without waving back.

I wasn't used to having anyone not like me. Well, more accurately, I didn't care when people didn't like me. I used to care a lot, but getting tied up in knots about other people's feelings was a waste of good energy.

But with Clint I cared. A lot.

And I needed to figure out why so I could make it stop.

CHAPTER 6

CLINT

S tanding outside the barn, I watched as Joji directed the movers. The two guys—who probably couldn't carry a full load of groceries on a good day—looked confused. It was good I brought Tyler and Dallas over to help. When they agreed, they had no idea what they were getting roped into.

My plan was to stay out of the way. Originally, I was going to muck the stalls, but Joji would need to know how to do that, so that chore could wait a day or two. Watching was much too entertaining.

Her hands moved constantly as she pointed this way and that, shouting instructions.

I was far enough away that she might not notice me watching. If she did, I'd end up taking orders just like the other guys. Considering she made me laugh, helping might not be so bad. But I had a gruff exterior to maintain.

Being around her was making it harder to keep up the crusty shell.

When Joji motioned toward the barn, I stepped out of

sight. Now was as good a time as any to refill the food containers with the right mix.

In the storage stall, I measured out the black oil sunflower seeds, alfalfa, barley, and other goodies.

The barn door opened, but I stayed out of the way, listening.

"We'll just . . . hmm. I'm not sure where to put it. I guess just put it right here in the middle." Joji was still being Napoleonic.

Dallas laughed. "Are you sure about that?"

"It doesn't fit in the house or the garage. This will at least keep it out of the weather."

Fighting the temptation to look, I scooped corn and added it to the feed.

"I'm not sure Clint would like that idea." Tyler sounded skeptical.

Now that my name had been brought up, I couldn't ignore what was happening.

"What's all the fuss about?" I stepped out of the stall and stopped.

A huge leopard-print sofa sat in the middle of the barn, set up like a viewing spot for milking.

Joji spun around, her eyes narrow. "No fuss. The couch didn't fit in the house."

"It doesn't go in here either." Barns were not intended to have couches in the middle.

"It's not *your* barn." Her hands moved to her hips, and anger flamed in her eyes. "Do you have a better idea?"

The piece was hideous. "Burn it."

This was the first sign of a redheaded temper, and instead of backing off and letting her cool down—which would have been the smart thing to do—I poured fuel on the blaze.

One of her eyebrows quirked upward. "Maybe I shouldn't

worry about the weather. Think the goats would like it in the pasture with them?"

Tyler and Dallas inched their way toward the barn door.

I stepped closer to Joji. "Be sure to put it near the fence because when Boingo gets out, the other goats can use the couch to follow him over."

For a couple of heartbeats, she stared at me. "Leave it here. I'll sell it."

I probably shouldn't have laughed.

Ignoring me, she followed the guys out of the barn. "Thank you so much for all the help. I couldn't have done it without you. Let me grab my purse."

"We were happy to help. No need to pay us." Tyler was kind that way.

Dallas would complain about it later.

I finished mixing the feed.

"I owe you, Clint." Joji peeked into the stall. When had she snuck back into the barn?

"You owe me for what?"

"Tyler and Dallas were so much help. I sent them back to the ranch. The movers are leaving." She pulled folded bills out of her pocket. "Give this to them. They wouldn't accept it from me."

I shoved the money into my pocket. "All done?"

"There is some furniture to move around in the house, but I can handle that." She flashed a muscle man pose with her arms bent at the elbow.

I tried to imagine her shoving a dresser around her bedroom. "I thought you'd been traveling and staying with friends. But that truck was full of stuff."

"I had a house in California. I sold it and put everything in storage when I set out on my world tour." She flopped onto the sofa. "I'd forgotten what the couch looked like."

"World tour, huh?"

"I visited lots of places. Not quite the whole world." She was arguably the most interesting woman I'd ever met. But she had horrible taste in couches.

"And then you bought a goat farm?"

She jumped up and slid her hands into the back pockets of her jeans. "Another day. Another adventure."

I'd never understand why she thought goat farming was an adventure. "Well, I'll be back this evening . . . unless you need something."

She grinned. "To me, that sounded like you were offering to help."

Shrugging, I stood. "If you need it."

"Not right now, but I'll keep it in mind." Walking toward the door, she glanced back over her shoulder. "I'm starting to wonder about you. I think your crusty exterior is all an act."

"Believe whatever you want."

When she reached the barn door, she spun around, reached up, and poked my chest. "It bothers me that you don't like me. And I aim to change that." What crazy scheme did she have in mind?

Telling her I didn't hate her would've ruined the fun. "Good luck with that."

THAT EVENING WHEN I ARRIVED, the barn was open. Either Joji was here waiting for me, or I'd be chasing goats for hours. The blaring music suggested she was here.

I stopped at the door and peeked in, hoping to catch her dancing again.

But no.

The woman was wrapping the sofa with plastic wrap. I'd never seen a box so big.

"I'm pretty sure that's not what plastic wrap is for."

"If guys can use duct tape for everything, I can use plastic wrap to protect the couch. I found Boingo on it earlier. That goat gets into everything."

"That's why we moved them outside. Those two back stalls open to the outside, but Boingo kept jumping out and eating the feed. So we closed the doors and built shelters. It's easier with him outside."

"I have a buyer interested." She glanced at the box as the last of the plastic wrap rolled off the cardboard tube. "Thankfully, Ava let me have this roll."

"Someone wants this couch?"

She tossed the box to the side and started yanking milking supplies out of cabinets. "It's nice."

"If a leopard wants a place to nap while camouflaged."

She set the milking pail on the stand. "You hate goats, animal print, and me. What do you like?"

"Quiet."

She slipped her phone out of her pocket and turned down the music. "Sorry."

"I never said I hated you. Animal print looks fine on animals. And goats remind me of a time in my life I'd rather forget." Why was I telling her that?

Facing away from me, she paused a second, then went back to getting out the supplies. "You milk Maude. I'll be back out to help feed the little guys in a bit."

Instead of explaining that she was supposed to be learning how to do it, I let her walk away.

Not surprisingly, I'd stuck my foot in my mouth and made her mad. But surprisingly, I wasn't sure which of my sentences bothered her. So much for sharing my feelings. I wouldn't make that mistake again.

The music shut off as she walked out of the barn. I milked Maude, then moved her back to her pen.

Joji was waiting when I walked back inside the barn. "I

put a pot of coffee on. After we bottle feed the boys, will you come inside and have a cup?"

The woman wanted to talk. That idea held about as much appeal as jumping out of a perfectly good airplane. "I should get back."

Her shoulders sagged. "Okay."

The normally chatty Joji filled the bottles in silence.

I needed to work on my people skills.

CHAPTER 7

JOJI

*D*inner was just about ready, and my friend Josefina would arrive any minute. I couldn't wait to show her around. I'd been unpacking for two days, and the place at least looked livable.

A knock echoed. The thin door didn't give off a satisfying thud. As I ran to open it, I heard Josefina fussing.

"Git. Don't eat my purse."

Boingo had become such a flirt. Anytime a female stepped onto the property, that goat was out of his pen.

"Hi! Sorry about Boingo. He's a pest. Drop your purse inside, then I'll show you the barn when I take him back to his pen."

"He's cute though. I'm sure he'll be popular with the ladies if you follow through with the goat yoga idea."

"I plan to. I just need to find an instructor who is willing to come out and teach classes."

"Maybe the promise of meeting cowboys will generate some interest." Josefina danced her eyebrows. She knew how I felt about boots and Wranglers.

"The ranch hands rarely get over this way. The only cowboy around here is Clint, and he's more of an acquired taste."

She tilted her head back, laughing. "And let me guess. You've acquired a taste?"

"Nothing like that. We are like night and day. And did I mention that he hates me? That irritates me."

"Why? I've seen you dancing like no one was watching when there was a large crowd gathered. You never care what people think." She stopped outside the barn. "What's going on with you two?"

"Those people were strangers. And I wish I could explain why it bothers me. I haven't figured it out yet." I yanked open the barn door. "There are goats in three separate pens. The baby goats are here in the barn. And there are two pens in the back. Guys and gals."

Josefina peeked into the stall. "They are so cute."

"They are. I'm glad I bought this place. These goats needed someone to take care of them." I led Boingo back to his pen.

"Want something else to take care of?"

"Such as?" I could see my little farm being filled with rescues.

"Kittens. A stray showed up at the house, and I fed her. Little did I know she was about to have kittens."

"You don't want them?"

"Mateo is allergic. I never should've fed the stray."

"Has anything changed with Mateo?" I wasn't sure why the two of them hadn't married already.

"We're still seeing each other. I'm just not sure I want more than that."

I rolled my eyes with enough drama to draw a laugh. "I'll take all the cats. Mama and the babies."

She grinned. "Thanks. Now, back to this Clint fella. Why do you think he hates you?"

"Because he hates redheads." I yanked at the end of a curl.

Mischief glimmered in her eyes. "So . . . don't be a redhead."

"I'm not going to color my hair just to make a man like me." Indignant at the thought, I slammed the barn door. "Seriously. You know me better than that."

"I wasn't suggesting anything permanent. And I doubt he hates you. But it's one way you could test the theory."

Intrigued by the idea and curious about how Clint would react, I couldn't dismiss her suggestion outright. "When you and I met, we just hit it off. From the first day, I knew we'd be friends. I felt that with Clint, but he won't even have coffee with me."

She shook her head. "I think you need to go out dancing again. We need to do something to get your mind off being hated by Clint."

"We should. But getting up early each morning puts a wrinkle in those plans. Let me get used to the routine around here, then we can schedule something. Come on. Let's go back to the house. I'm hungry."

While I ladled soup into bowls, Josefina poured two glasses of wine. "Did you order a new couch? You mentioned you were looking for one."

"I did. It should be here by the weekend. And I have someone coming to get the other couch tomorrow."

She laid a napkin in her lap. "I can't believe you wrapped that entire thing in plastic wrap. Who bought it?"

"Some woman who writes romance novels. She doesn't live that far away. Just down the road in Stadtburg."

"What time tomorrow? Maybe I'll drop off the kitties about that time so I can see who needed a leopard print couch."

I laughed. "That thing is awful. I'm not sure what I was thinking when I bought it. That was in my wild phase."

"And this is your calm phase?"

"Exactly." I couldn't even get the word out without giggling. My wild stage would likely last forever.

THE ROBUST AROMA of strong coffee filled the kitchen as I filled two mugs. It reminded me of the café in Paris where I spent hours watching people. In all the places I visited, I always made time to watch people. And it was always interesting—how they walked, what they ate, who attracted their attention.

At the ranch when I'd had lunch in the mess hall, I'd watched everyone. Clint had the respect of those guys. What had that man so closed off? It had to be related to the redhead who left him. I didn't even know her, and I wanted to pull her hair out.

I added a splash of cream and two sugar cubes to my cup but left the other coffee black. Clint didn't seem like the cream and sugar type.

This was my experiment, my way of ascertaining if Clint was averse to coffee or the conversation that often accompanied it when sitting at a table. There was less risk in standing around and drinking coffee in the barn. Right?

Josefina's idea about not being a redhead still noodled its way through my thoughts, but I hadn't decided on that one yet.

Carrying two mugs, I smiled as Clint climbed out of his truck. "Morning. I brought you a cup of coffee. What do you take in it?"

He stuffed his keys in his pocket. "Nothing."

Happy I'd guessed correctly, I handed over the mug of black coffee. "Anything new today?"

He sipped his coffee. "Strong. The way I like it."

Why didn't that surprise me?

"You run through the routine this morning. I'll watch." He pulled open the barn door.

"You mean supervise?"

His lips curled into a smile.

Magic beans were real. Thanks to the coffee, his smile had materialized.

After downing half my cup, I set the mug aside and gathered what I needed, reciting my rhyme as I did.

"Any progress on your goat yoga idea?"

The coffee even had Clint making conversation.

And his smile had me feeling like I was winning the day.

"I need to find an instructor. Maybe I'll dangle the possibility of meeting a cowboy."

"You bring a yoga instructor around these parts, and I'm guessing the ranch hands will find reasons to show up while class is going on."

"I'll let you know when I need you to spread the word."

He hadn't mentioned wearing stretching pants or participating, but since he'd actually smiled today, I decided not to bring up those topics.

I milked Maude, cleaned up the stand, then carried the pail of milk inside after pouring off enough for the baby goats. When I made it back to the barn, Clint was feeding both goats.

With one tucked under each arm, he held the bottles up, managing to hold their chins at just the right angle. There was no way the man hated goats.

After watching silently a minute, I stepped into the stall. "You're pretty good at this."

"I grew up on a goat farm."

Connecting his comment to what he'd said yesterday, I thought of a hundred other questions, then bit my tongue. "You're clearly a natural."

He shrugged. "If you want to feed the other goats outside, I'll finish up here."

That was my cue to stop watching him. I backed away and fed the other goats. So far, today had been a good day.

CHAPTER 8

CLINT

*B*ringing me coffee was a poorly veiled attempt to get me talking. Why did she care why I hated goats or why I avoided redheads . . . or most women for that matter? But saying no to a cup of coffee would've been rude. And being rude to Joji seemed like an inexcusable sort of rudeness.

The surprise of it all was that Joji's coffee was ten times better than what Ava served. Maybe even good enough to endure conversation.

I'd just finished feeding the kids when the barn door swung open.

"Helloooooo." A woman only slightly taller than Joji but a couple of decades older sashayed into the barn.

I stepped out of the stall. "Can I help you?"

She fanned herself. "Oh my, yes. If I call my photographer right now, will you let her take pictures of you for my book cover?"

The woman made Joji look normal.

"Not a chance." I pushed open the back door of the barn. "Trouble, are you expecting someone?"

"Oh! It must be the woman getting the couch." Joji wiped her hands on the back of her jeans as she ran in. "Tandy?"

"Yes! Hello, dear. Before we settle up on this beautiful couch, will you introduce me to your cowboy?"

That was my cue to exit the building. I tipped my hat and strode out of the barn. "Have a nice day. I'll be back this evening."

The last thing I heard was Joji.

"That's Clint. He's a bit shy."

That was one way of putting it.

Two steps away from the barn, I was accosted by another woman. Well, she waved and ran up to me.

"Hi. I'm Josefina, Joji's friend. I stopped by to drop off these kittens." She balanced a box on her hip and stuck out her hand. "You must be Clint."

"I am. It's nice to meet you. Joji's in the barn with the woman buying the sofa." That was when it hit me that they'd need help loading. I slid my phone out of my pocket. "I'm going to get one of the other guys to head over so we can load it." I hoped that Tandy woman had a truck because there was no way I was going to deliver it to her house.

Josefina smiled. "You are just like Joji described you. I'm guessing she doesn't intend to leave these tiny kittens in the barn. Would you mind putting them in the house?"

"Sure. I guess." I peeked inside the box when she handed it over.

Of course Joji would take in seven cats.

How had I let myself get wrangled into going inside? I'd made a point to stay out of the house since she moved her stuff in. But I couldn't exactly move that couch while holding kittens. I also wasn't moving that couch alone. And I wouldn't get help if I didn't ask for it.

Which of the guys wouldn't be bothered by Tandy's gawking?

Hidalgo. Dag could handle Tandy. And that green-eyed cowboy would keep her attention off me.

Standing on the porch, I dialed his number.

Dag answered right away. "What's up, boss?"

"I'm at Joji's. I could use your help loading an ugly couch into a"—I scanned the parking area to see what that Tandy woman was driving—"a pickup."

"Be there in two shakes."

"All right, cats. Now to figure out what to do with you."

Joji's front door creaked as I pushed it open. Next time I was over this way, I'd bring a can of WD-40.

The place looked vastly different with her stuff in it. With all that was out on display—art and knick-knacks from around the world—I wondered what she planned to do with what was still in the stacked boxes.

"Where should I put you so you won't get into things?" If I set the box in the living room, those cats would be all over the place by the time Joji came back inside.

The bathroom seemed the most logical place.

That door creaked as it swung open. I had my work cut out for me.

She'd embraced the black and white flooring in here. The bathroom was decorated like a 1950s diner. But the see-through shower curtain didn't seem at all practical. Neither did the bras dangling from the shower bar. Lacy, but not practical.

I set the box on the floor, made sure the toilet lid was down, and walked out, only glancing back once.

It wasn't the cats that had my attention.

Just as the door rattled against the frame, I winced. The kittens were too little to jump. But that mama cat could be dangling off Joji's pretty things with one good leap. I picked up the box and headed toward the other bathroom, which meant going through her bedroom. This was a bad plan.

Focused on the bathroom door, trying to ignore the plush comforter and open drawers, I made my way through the room. The master bathroom had just as many bras hanging from the bar, and there were undergarments on the floor. Even the kittens could ruin those.

Why had I said yes to bringing the box inside?

I walked the box of cats back to the front bathroom, and after setting it down, I inhaled. Without taking more time to think about it, I yanked the bras off the bar.

With bras dangling from one hand, I hurried down the hall, then dropped them on the kitchen counter as I walked toward the front door.

Hopefully, Joji wouldn't ask how they got there.

Dag pulled up as I stepped onto the porch.

I needed to warn him about Tandy before those women emerged from the barn. "Thanks for coming. The woman buying the couch is—"

That Tandy woman squealed.

Too late.

"Oh wow! Another cowboy. Joji, you are going to be my new best friend if I'm guaranteed to see these guys whenever I come over."

Dag flashed a wide smile and stuck out his hand. "Hidalgo Gonzales. Most people call me Dag."

Tandy wiggled her fingers. "Just looking at you, I feel a story coming on. And you have charm. That other cowboy hardly said a word."

"Clint is the silent type." Dag laughed before glancing over his shoulder at me, panic etched on his face.

Tandy had that effect on men, I guess.

"Let's get that couch loaded." As soon as I was done loading, I could be on my way.

A hand brushed against mine. I turned to my left to see Joji smiling up at me.

"Thanks for getting help. I hadn't thought that far ahead."

"No problem." I shoved my hands in my pockets because I didn't need her fingers touching my skin anymore. "Why don't you move the truck up by the barn door, and we'll get it loaded?"

Dag disappeared inside the barn. I'd never seen him so spooked.

With a little wrangling and too much advice from the spectators, Dag and I loaded the sofa and tied it down.

"Well, if that's all you need . . . Dag and I will be on our way."

Tandy rubbed her hands together. "What I need or what I want?"

My good manners barely winning out, I asked one more question. "Will you have help getting it unloaded?"

Dag shot me a look that made it clear he did not want to be volunteered.

"My neighbor. A gorgeous hunk of a man. I can say that because his wife isn't here glaring at me." Tandy danced her eyebrows. "Hank will help me."

"I'm not sure one person can move it alone." I didn't envy Hank.

"He has a deputy friend who is just as good looking. He can help."

Joji popped her hands on her hips and rose to her full height—all four feet eleven inches. "Hank Sparks?"

Tandy nodded. "You know him?"

"He's my nephew." Joji's stare would make anyone uncomfortable.

"Oops. Small world. I should be more careful with what I say." Tandy didn't seem the least bit sorry.

Joji pressed a hand to my back and nudged me toward my truck. "Thanks for all your help. It's greatly appreciated."

I tipped my hat out of habit. "See you later."

She dropped her voice to a whisper and leaned in close. "My favorite thing about evenings."

Tandy was rubbing off on Joji, and that wasn't a good thing.

"I hope you don't start keeping regular company with that woman."

Joji ran her fingers through her curls. "We'll see." Hips swaying from side to side, she walked back toward the barn.

All I could think about was the lace on her counter and on her bathroom floor.

Joji's purple beast wasn't around when I arrived at the barn that evening. I'd start without her.

Gathering the needed items for milking, I tried to remember her rhyme. Working with her wasn't too bad so far . . . except for all the touching. The worst part of that was, I liked it.

Working on the ranch, I could go days without someone shaking my hand or slapping my shoulder. But almost every time I showed up here, she'd make contact somehow. And I was starting to look forward to it.

As I locked Maude into the milking stand, Joji burst into the barn. "So sorry I'm late. I had to run into town to get stuff for the cats. The selection of pet supplies in Stadtburg was limited, so I drove into San Antonio. I had no idea it would take so long."

"Don't worry about it."

She eased up next to me and bumped her shoulder against my side. "I can milk her. You supervise."

I stepped aside.

She hummed as she worked. Then she stopped and

glanced at me. "Did I tell you—never mind." Focused on Maude, she went back to milking.

"Tell me what?"

"It's not important." She hummed a second, then fell silent.

Until now, she'd chattered through nearly every milking session. Having her quiet felt wrong especially since I was fairly sure it was because I'd said I liked quiet.

If she didn't intend to make conversation, I would. "Goats aren't enough work for you?"

"What do you mean?"

"You haven't even been moved in a week, and you adopted cats."

"Josefina couldn't keep them. They needed a home." She wiped Maude down before letting the goat out of the stand. "And I have room out here."

"Taking in strays. Why doesn't that surprise me?"

She turned as she walked out the back door. "I'm nearly fifty and still single. I think it's a requirement that I own a mess of cats."

I hadn't figured out how she'd managed to stay single so long.

When Joji walked up next to me, I continued filling the baby bottles. "What were you going to tell me?"

"Tandy writes romance novels." She bounced on the balls of her feet as if excited to share the news.

"Of course she does. If I show up as a character in one of her books, let me know."

"You'll read it?"

"Not a chance." I handed her a bottle. "You still need to name these little guys."

"I'll work on that. I have to name the cats too. Inspiration hasn't hit."

"It'll be a busy week." I watched as she wrangled one of the kids into position. Even next to the little goat, Joji looked pint sized.

She caught me staring. "Thanks for keeping kitty claws off my lace."

And now I wanted it quiet.

She studied me a second before speaking again. "What's the story with the trailer? I need to get in there and see what it's like."

"Ava cleaned it out a few months back. The old owner had it brought in after her husband died." I was thankful for the change in conversation.

"Do I want to know why?" Joji crinkled her nose.

"She thought her husband was haunting the house, so she moved into the trailer."

"Haunted, huh? That's just what I need."

"I'm pretty sure your place isn't haunted."

And even if it were, Joji seemed like she could handle almost anything.

"Do you believe a place can be haunted?"

I turned my focus back to the goat. "Not sure about places. But I believe people can be haunted by whatever voices they let live in their head."

Her silence surprised me, and after a few seconds I glanced up. She flashed a soft smile, one that hinted she knew firsthand about voices in her head.

"I think you're right. But I might buy some sage just in case." Her copper curls danced as she laughed. "I'm not sure what to do with it though."

She didn't seem afraid, but was she masking fear with humor?

The only way to know was to ask. "Worried you aren't safe?"

"With you around? Not a chance. I have your number, remember?"

And there wasn't a chance I'd forget.

CHAPTER 9

JOJI

or a week, I'd soaked up information each morning and evening and unpacked boxes in between. After our one good morning and evening, Clint had been extra quiet. It wasn't for lack of coffee.

I gave him a cup every morning. And limiting my chatter hadn't done much to change his mood either. At times, he seemed almost irritated that I was quiet.

I wasn't one for changing based on someone's opinion, but biting my tongue a little wasn't going to hurt me. He was kind enough to teach me about goat farming. I could keep a few extra thoughts inside my head.

Josefina's idea would have to wait another day. Last night as Clint climbed into the truck, he'd warned me that today we'd be mucking the barn, which sounded like a nasty job. He'd put off the job a couple of weeks so that I had time to unpack.

Even when Clint was grumpy, he was thoughtful. The man was a riddle.

I yanked on my boots as the rumble of his truck sounded outside.

I'd miss it when he stopped coming over every morning. Considering I did all the chores, and he mostly supervised, that day was closer than I wanted it to be.

Before walking out the door, I filled two mugs with coffee.

"Morning." I handed him his cup. "How are you today?"

"Better now. Don't tell Ava, but you make the best coffee." He dragged the tip of his boot through the dirt. "I figure after another couple of weeks, you won't need me coming over every day, but I'll still check in once a week or so."

I started a countdown in my head. Drawing sad faces on my calendar would be too obvious.

"Do you have a bandana?" He opened the barn door as he always did.

"For?"

"Covering your mouth when we muck out the stall. You don't want to be breathing in that stuff."

"I don't have one. Would a dishtowel work?"

He laughed. "As much as I'd like to see you with a dishtowel tied around your head, I think this will be more comfortable." He handed me a red bandana. "I brought an extra just in case."

"You're sweet."

"That can be our little secret." He stopped before opening the cabinet. "Are you going to say the rhyme?"

I recited the lines as we pulled out what we needed. Then we ran through the routine. The morning chores were becoming second nature, and today it was more of a team effort.

"When do you think would be a good time to add more goats to the farm?"

Clint shrugged and walked Maude back to her pen.

Just when I thought he didn't hate me, he reverted to the crusty guy who'd shown up on day one.

I followed him outside. "Does that shrug mean you don't think it's a good idea for me to get more goats?"

"Didn't say that. It's your place. Do what you want."

"I intend to." I let the door slam as I stormed back into the barn. Why was I throwing a mini tantrum?

He grabbed a shovel after tying a bandana so that it covered his nose and mouth.

"You look like you're back in the Old West about to rob a train." I yanked the red bandana out of my back pocket.

"Why are you mad?"

"I'm not." I fiddled with the fabric corners, trying to get them tied.

Clint leaned the shovel against the wall, then stepped behind me. "Let me help you." His warm fingers brushed against mine as he grabbed the bandana. "I wasn't trying to start a fight."

His soothing tone made me feel like a toddler.

"Why didn't you just answer my question?"

"I think maybe I mentioned that I don't like goats. Why would I suggest you get more?" He moved away and closed the little goats into one of the other stalls.

"Oh."

"We're going to shovel the hay out of the stall. Then we'll move it again . . . into the trailer just outside. Dag will bring over the four-wheeler when he's done with it, and we'll haul the mess out to the compost pile."

"Where's that?"

"Far corner of the property."

"Is there a lot of compost?"

"Why?" His eyebrows pinched together.

"Because I'm thinking about planting a garden. And I'll need a good amount of compost to mix in with the soil."

"There's plenty for a garden. Shoot. You could plant ten gardens and have enough."

"Yay. I plan to wait until the spring to plant. I could do a fall garden, but I don't know much about that. Not that I know much about growing anything at all." I picked up the other shovel. "Do you know anything about gardening?"

"A little." He shoveled the nasty hay and straw out of the stall.

Next to him, I started doing the same. "I can't figure out why you are so closed off. It's like you don't want to have friends."

"I have a friend."

"Beau?"

"Yep. One good friend seems like plenty." He traded the shovel for a rake and pulled hay and straw out of the corners.

"One friend? What about Ava?"

"She's my sister."

"Lilith?"

"Beau's girl." Clint had an answer for everything.

"So, what about the ranch hands?"

"I'm their boss." He stopped shoveling and turned to face me. "Any other questions?"

"What about me?" I held his gaze, hoping he wouldn't walk right out of the barn.

His mouth moved like he was chewing the inside of his lip. "I haven't figured that out yet."

Did that mean there was a chance we could be friends? I wanted to hope so. "We should get back to work. I'm guessing we'll have to do the outside pens also."

"The space under the shelters."

We worked in silence for what seemed like an eternity. The quiet bothered me. How could he like it?

"Do you shave every morning?"

He shot me a side glance. "Yep."

"Have you ever skipped shaving for a day or two?" I really

wondered what his boyish face would look like covered in whiskers.

"Every November."

I had something to look forward to.

Shoveling, we fell into a rhythm, and we finished in short order.

"I have clean straw in the back of the truck. I'll lay it down in here, then we can either move this to the trailer or work outside."

"Whatever you think is best, boss."

His jaw tensed. "We'll move this pile to the trailer."

I watched as he laid down straw. So far, running this place wasn't impossible. I was tired at the end of each day, but eager to start again the next morning.

That had nothing to do with Clint.

Sweaty and tired, I followed Clint to Boingo's pen.

He glanced back. "Close the gate. I don't feel like chasing these guys."

"I learned that lesson on day one." I scanned the pen. "You still haven't taught me all the names."

"Remind me about it tomorrow. It's getting hot, and I want to finish." He looked from the shelter to the fence. "I'm going to pull the trailer up next to the fence. I'll bring a bucket, and we can cut the job in half."

"Whatever you say, b—"

He spun around, and there was no sign of humor on his face. "Quit calling me that."

"Yes, sir." I had to bite my lip to keep from laughing. Was I slowly winning him over or just irritating the poor man? Why did he care if I called him boss? Now probably wasn't the best time to ask.

I fanned myself, waiting for him to get back. Boingo bounded up, wanting a scratch.

"*You* like me, don't you?" Talking to a goat didn't make me look crazy at all.

"Here." Clint handed me a five-gallon bucket. "Shovel stuff into here, then dump it into the trailer." He set his bucket down.

As he turned to face me, I leaned forward to put mine beside his. Something hard and goat-like slammed into my backside, launching me forward. Time slowed down just like in the cartoons.

The shovel flew out of my hand. I said a word my mother would've considered naughty. Then I braced for impact. Gravity pulled my face toward the bucket, and no amount of grabbing at the air would change the inevitable.

The bucket skittered away as Clint dove toward the ground like he was sliding into home plate . . . except he was on his back.

I landed face first against his chest. His broad chest.

Sprawled half on top of Clint, I waited an extra second before lifting my head.

This was an even better treat than when he'd helped me out of the tree. And I hadn't even had to climb.

His hand slid down my back. "You okay?"

When had he wrapped his arms around me?

I picked up my head just enough to look him in the face. Getting up close and personal with Clint was an added perk of buying the goat farm.

The man had a nice chest. His arms weren't bad either. And even closing in on fifty, I appreciated a nice physique.

How long could I stay here before it got weird? Who was I kidding? This was weirder than weird. Based on the way Ava and Lilith talked about him, this was probably the closest he'd been to a woman in a long while.

"Thanks for throwing yourself on the ground to save me.

But maybe just grabbing me would have been a better option."

"There wasn't much space between your head and that bucket. I didn't have a lot of time to think about it." He winced when he shifted.

"Are you hurt?"

"I'm fine. I should've warned you about Bumpo. It's best not to bend over when he's near." He let his arm slide off my back. "You sure you're okay?"

"I think I'm fine. But I think this pen is cursed. This is the second time you've had to save me from crashing into the ground."

"How would it make me look if I let you get hurt?" A door slammed, and Clint's eyes widened. "That's probably Dag."

I pushed off his chest and scrambled to my feet.

Rubbing my backside, I stuck out my tongue at Bumpo. "I won't forget this."

"Are you talking to the goat or to me?" Clint shot a nervous glance toward Dag's pickup.

"Both."

I leaned down to pick up my shovel, but Clint grabbed my arm.

"I'll get it. Bumpo looks ready to give a repeat performance."

"Did you name him?"

Clint shook his head. "Sutton, the guy who used to take care of the goat farm, named these goats." He pointed at Bumpo. "This guy started that bad habit when he was really little." Eying the goats, Clint reached down and picked up the shovels. "I can take care of this if you need to sit."

"Sitting might hurt. Besides, I need to be able to do this stuff."

"Why don't we finish the job tomorrow? You go relax."

I didn't want to be pampered. Okay, maybe I did a little, but I needed to be able to run this place . . . alone. "Would you say the same thing if one of the ranch hands had gotten bumped?"

"You aren't one of the ranch hands. And"—he tucked his chin and waggled his finger—"you don't have anything to prove. Not to me or anybody. This hay will still be nasty tomorrow. Don't be a martyr." He crossed his arms, daring me to argue.

"That was a lot of words coming from you."

"Can you walk, or do you need me to carry you?"

It was shocking that he'd offered with one of the ranch hands around. And Clint's half smile made me want to call his bluff. But being in his arms right now was a horrible idea. All the reasons why were unclear, but I followed my gut instinct.

"I'll walk." My butt ached, and each passing minute made it worse. Trying not to hobble, I trudged out of the pen, letting Clint close the gate.

"Dag, I'll help you unload that in just a sec." Clint stayed beside me until I reached my front door. "Need anything?"

"Pain pills and a hot bath." I ran my fingers through my curls, pulling out stray pieces of hay. "I'm a mess."

"I can get you pain pills, but I can't help with the bath. I'll circle back a bit later and check in."

Channeling my inner Tandy, I propped a fist on my hip. "Can't or won't?"

"Take your pick." He tipped his hat. "Feel better. If you need something, call me."

The dirt and debris all down his back showed off Clint's selfless side. He obviously didn't hate me. But it was too soon to hope for more.

Three steps away from the porch, he stopped. "You're tougher than you look."

"Thanks for saying so."

He smiled as he turned.

How was he going to explain the scene in the pen to Dag? That was an explanation I wanted to hear.

CHAPTER 10

CLINT

*D*ag eyed me as I limped toward the truck. I'd landed harder than anticipated. Sore muscles would be my reward for breaking Joji's fall. Well, sore muscles and that look she gave me.

His timing couldn't have been more perfect because the temptation to kiss Joji pounded in my chest with her so close.

"You're limping, and you have blood on your arm." He smoothed his hair before setting his Stetson on his head.

"Bumpo executed an attack. Let's get this out of the truck, then we should head back to the ranch. I'm guessing the hay arrived."

"They were still waiting for it when I left." Dag let down the tailgate. "Are we going to talk about how you two were on the ground tangled in each other's arms?"

"I already told you what happened." The last thing I needed were rumors getting around.

Beau would have a field day if he thought there were any sparks between the redhead and me. That was reason enough not to kiss her.

Why did I keep thinking about kissing her?

"Bumpo explains how you got onto the ground but not why you were in that compromising situation smiling at each other like teens."

"There's nothing to talk about." I used my boss voice. "To anyone."

"You got it, boss." Dag laughed. "I'll keep your little secret."

"There's no secret."

We unloaded the four-wheeler, then Dag climbed into his truck. "I need to check on the windmill. I'll be back at the barn later."

"Thanks for bringing this over." I glanced at Joji's house as I walked to my truck.

The idea of a hot bath held appeal, but I had work to do. I fished pain medicine out of my glovebox and swallowed down two. That would have to do until I had time for a hot shower . . . or an ice pack. Right now, there was hay to be stacked.

Seven minutes later, I pulled up outside the barn and yanked on my gloves as I climbed out of the truck. The load of hay had been delivered, and unloading and stacking was always a big job.

Beau eyed me as I set to work. He'd been handling most of the daily operations, but I tried to be around as much as possible. After what had just happened, focusing on my ranch duties proved to be a challenge.

Talking about what needed to be done would get my mind off Joji. Maybe. "Have you made that vet appointment?" Handing off tasks made me uneasy. I worried something would get missed.

He nodded. "Called the new one who joined the large animal practice in Stadtburg. I've heard good things about her."

Having another woman on the ranch begged for trouble. If it weren't for those kindergarten goat-watching tours, we'd still have Sutton working for us, and Beau wouldn't have sold the goat farm to Joji.

I suppose I had a kindergarten teacher to thank for Joji's arrival.

"What happened to you?" Beau startled me with his question.

How did he know that anything happened? Surely, Joji hadn't called Ava already. Had Dag said something? Had there even been enough time for the story to spread?

"What?"

"The blood on your elbow. And the back of your shirt and jeans are a mess."

"I'm fine. Took a tumble at Joji's." I desperately tried to keep a casual tone.

Beau lifted another bale and slung it onto the stack. "All joking aside, I appreciate you helping Miss Sparks with the goat farm. Think she'll stick around? It's a lot of work, and she's never been around animals."

Picturing the determination in her eyes, I had no doubt she'd stick around. "She seems to be taking to it."

"Too bad she's a redhead. Otherwise, maybe she could've been your happily ever after." That was the Beau I knew.

"On a goat farm? Very funny." I flung another bale onto the pile without making eye contact with Beau.

Once the hay was where it needed to be, I snuck off to take a shower. I couldn't remember the last time I'd done that in the middle of the day. But if I showed up at lunch with blood on my arm, Ava would ask questions.

And of all the people I could bluff, my sister wasn't one of them.

I arrived at the dining hall before the rest of the guys made an appearance. "Smells good in here."

"Fried chicken." Ava wiped her hands on her apron. "How are you? Hurting?"

Trying to quell my panic, I picked up two plates. "I guess you talked to Joji."

Ava narrowed her eyes, and a smile played on her lips. "No, I talked to Beau, but you can bet your best pair of boots I'll be calling Joji." She tore off a large piece of foil. "I hope the story she'll tell me is a good story, and not one where you are making her feel like she doesn't belong on a ranch."

"Why would I do that?"

"Because when that billionaire down the road—Drake something or another—bought that spread, you went on for days about how money didn't make him a rancher. Don't give her a hard time about her money."

I hadn't much thought about Joji having money. "It's her money. She can do what she wants with it."

"She knows that. I seriously doubt she cares about your opinion."

"I'm sure she doesn't." I could always thank my sister for helping me see straight. The reminder that I was mostly irrelevant—which wasn't what Ava had intended; I knew her better than that—was exactly what I needed to help me focus. "What's the foil for?"

"You picked up two plates. I assumed you were taking one to Joji."

"Thanks. She fell this morning, so I'm going to check on her. Thought I'd take her a plate. But if you could get me another piece. I'll just take my plate to go."

"How nice of you. If she needs anything, tell her to call me."

"Will do." I carried both plates out of the dining room, ready to be far away from people who could read me.

Before pulling away from the house, I texted Joji. Who knew what I'd walk into if I showed up unannounced?

The cab of the truck smelled like my mama's kitchen by the time I arrived at Joji's place Not all memories from growing up were bad. Sunday lunch with a table full of fried chicken would always make me smile.

Balancing the plates in one hand, I knocked.

"It's open. Come in." Joji must really be hurting if she didn't even feel like walking to the door.

"I brought lunch. Ava made fried chicken." I blinked as I stepped into the dark house. "Still hurting?"

"Yes, and it's embarrassing. Every step radiates pain."

"He probably bruised your tailbone. I'll handle chores this evening." I stepped into the living room and froze.

Leaning back on the sofa, Joji brushed a long blonde hair out of her face. "Thanks for bringing food."

"What did you do?"

Mischief danced in her eyes. "I took a long hot bath, sat on an ice pack for a bit, then started watching one of those sweet romantic movies. Why?"

"Your hair. What did you do to it?" As much as I complained about redheads, I liked them. A lot. I just didn't like the temper that so often accompanied the fiery locks.

Joji didn't have that temperament.

But she was still a redhead. And every woman with fiery red hair dredged up pain, the kind I'd rather forget forever.

As the fog of the shock cleared, logic took over. "You didn't color it. It's too long. And if you have something that could grow hair that fast, you'd be richer than God. A wig?"

"You like it?"

"Not really. You want to eat here or at the table?"

She tapped her backside. "I won't be sitting in those wooden chairs for a few days." She moved her feet off the sofa and shifted to a sitting position. "I see a second plate. You going to keep me company while I eat?"

"I can do that." I eased onto the sofa, not wanting to jostle her. "But please take off that wig."

She pulled it off and shook her curls loose. "I know you don't like redheads. I thought this might make it easier for you."

"Nuttier than a fruitcake. Did I say that already?"

She laughed as she reached for the plate. "I'm beginning to think you don't hate me."

"I never said I hated you."

We were as different as night and day, but here I was having lunch with her when there were a hundred chores waiting for me.

All those chores would still be there after lunch.

CHAPTER 11

I wasn't sure what was bruised worse, my backside or my ego. But when Clint pulled up to the barn for the evening chores, I had everything ready and waiting.

He shook his head as he approached. "I said I'd handle it."

"I didn't buy this place just to have some handsome cowboy run it. I need to be able to take care of things, pain or no pain." I stared up at him, expecting him to argue.

"What did you say?" His ears turned red, and he rubbed the back of his neck.

I had to think through my mini speech. "You heard me. I need to be able to do this."

"That part I heard." One side of his mouth curled up. "And you're incredibly stubborn."

"You'd recognize that trait, wouldn't you?"

Maybe we weren't completely different. I flipped over a crate and stepped up so that I was almost eye level with him. "Please. Don't give me a hard time. If the pain gets to be too much, I'll say something."

His gaze dropped to the crate, and he smiled. "Maybe you

should put a string on that and use it to get in and out of your truck."

"That's a great idea. I think it would work. If I—" The crate teetered as I shifted my weight.

Clint had his hands on my waist quicker than a cat jumping out of a bathtub. And that was quick. I knew that for a fact because I'd tried to bathe kitty the other day.

"Please don't fall again."

"Just so you know, that only happens when you're around." I leaned into him as I stepped off.

All this time we were spending together stirred up feelings I wasn't prepared for. But with Clint there was no hope of romance. Entertaining those thoughts would only lead to heartache.

And I'd been single all my life. Romance had left me behind years ago.

Clint was, at best, friend material. And even that would take work.

Once my feet were safely on the ground, he let go. "I'll get Maude."

It had been a long time since I wanted a man close to me or since a guy's touch sent sparks—no pun intended—dancing up my spine.

As Clint locked Maude into the milking stand, I sat on the milking stool which was the worst decision I'd made all day. I tried to stifle my gasp.

Clint didn't say a word, but one eyebrow lifted slightly.

Back on my feet, I moved away from the stand. "If you don't mind, I'll let you milk her."

"I don't mind."

I bit my lip as I shifted and found a way to stand that didn't make it feel like someone was stabbing me in the butt. "You know a lot about goats. What can you tell me about chickens?"

"They taste good smoked, barbequed, roasted. And when I get takeout, I almost always get chicken with cashews. They pair well together." He didn't look up.

"Very funny. Listen to you with your 'they pair well together.' Are you one of those cowboy chefs?"

He shot me the side eye. "What do you think?"

"Probably not. Anyway, I was asking a serious question. While resting my bruised backside, I spent hours scrolling through social media. People have postings about free stuff. Anyway, there is a lady who is moving across country. She can't take her chickens with her. And she needs someone to take them."

He sucked in a deep breath. "When is she bringing them over?"

"Day after tomorrow. What do I need to get?"

He blew out that deep breath . . . slowly. "You are going to need a place to keep them."

"I was reading about that. Where can I buy a chicken coop?"

"Where do you want to put it?"

"I was hoping to get your advice on that." I eased up beside him and rested a hand on his shoulder. "How are you feeling? That was a hard fall."

"Better after a hot shower and some time with an icepack. The back of my shoulder is angry with me."

I rubbed his shoulder a little before dropping my hand. Those bees I'd stirred up on day one were all inside me, and touching this guy only made the buzz louder.

"About the chicken coop." Thinking about chickens might help me.

"I'll start building it in the morning. And after we feed the littles, we can figure out where to put it." As he wiped down Maude, he laughed. "Cats and now chickens. You'll adopt just about anything, won't you?"

"They need a home, and I have a place. I don't see a problem."

"I can't wait to see what you take in next."

As promised, Clint was hammering away as the sun came up.

I carried out a mug of coffee. "Good morning. I really didn't mean for you to go to all this work."

He shrugged as he accepted the cup. "Not a big deal."

"I'm making tomato and goat cheese toast for breakfast. Can I make you some?"

He set down his hammer. "Did you make the cheese?"

I held up my hands, wiggling my fingers. "With these two hands."

"Sure. I'll try it."

"Great. I'll let you know when it's ready." I hurried back inside as fast as my bruised tailbone allowed.

In a matter of minutes, I had several pieces of sourdough toasted, topped with goat cheese, tomato, fried egg, and basil. It didn't look anything like something Clint would eat. He was likely more a meat and potatoes kind of guy.

I stepped out onto the porch.

He stood and stretched. "Is it ready?"

"Yep. Why don't you come in and eat? Have another cup of coffee."

He picked up his mug and strode toward the house.

Once inside, he removed his cowboy hat and hung it on the hat rack mounted to the wall beside the door.

Not taking that down was a good call. But it was curious. The first few times he'd come inside, he'd set his hat on the counter closest to the door. This was the first time he'd used the hat rack.

Reading too much into him hanging his hat at my place was a bad idea. Did it stop me? No.

I set plates on the table and refilled his coffee cup. "I'm hoping that next year, I'll be able to walk outside and pick tomatoes and fresh basil."

"You going to start making your own bread?"

I watched as he took his first bite. "I made that loaf last night. I have this sourdough starter that just keeps growing. So if you ever want a loaf, let me know."

"Why weren't you resting last night?"

"I wasn't sitting in a wooden chair. It wasn't bad. But once I get the chickens, and they start laying eggs, I'll have one more of the ingredients I need to make this." I took a bite of my new favorite food. "I was trying to figure out what to do with goat cheese—because until I start selling it, I'm going to have quite a bit around here—and I made this. I've had it every morning since. Do you know how long it'll take the chickens to lay eggs? I read that moving can throw them off."

"I'm not sure." He wolfed down a second, third, and fourth slice of toast.

"Need more?"

"Maybe later." He picked up his plate and cup and walked into the kitchen. "But I think the goats can wait while I have one more cup of coffee."

"I'm sure they can. With the chickens, I've heard that if I sit out there and talk to them, it might help them feel more at home."

"I thought sitting was a problem." He glanced at my chair as he walked back to the table.

"A pillow does the trick. I'll just throw one in my foldout lawn chair and tell those chickens all about how I take care of the goats."

"They'll be thrilled, I'm sure."

My phone rang, and Clint jumped up to grab it off the counter. "It's Ava. Could you maybe . . . not mention . . ."

"Don't worry. I'll keep our relationship a secret."

His ears turned red. "That wasn't what I meant." Grabbing his hat, he turned to face me. "I get enough ribbing from the guys at the ranch."

We clearly weren't at the joking stage of friendship. Even calling it a friendship was a stretch.

He liked my coffee. And didn't seem to mind my wonderful goat cheese breakfast. I guess that made me like a diner . . . except he hung his hat by my door.

CHAPTER 12

CLINT

Watching Joji talk to goats was funny, and I didn't have much room to tease because I talked to them too. But the way she conversed with the chickens proved to be a whole new level of hysterical.

I'd finished the chicken coop with only a little time to spare, and when the chickens arrived, Joji plopped herself in a lawn chair equipped with a pillow and told her new feathered friends all about the farm.

Pretending not to listen, I hung around to do the evening chores.

I finished them in record time, then walked back over to the chicken coop. "They seem more relaxed."

"Make fun all you want. I'm hoping for eggs soon."

I admired her determination, however creative her methods were. "You coming to the ranch for dinner? Ava said you're welcome anytime."

Adding the part about Ava helped gloss over the fact that I'd done the asking.

"I think I'm just going to make myself more of that toast.

And I called a woman today about teaching yoga classes out here. I'm hoping she calls back."

"Have fun. Holler if you need anything." I climbed into the truck. As I started the engine, she walked up to my window.

She crossed her arms. "I can handle the morning chores. If there's a problem, I'll text you."

Without a doubt she could handle it, but I wasn't ready to stop seeing her every morning. Admitting it to myself tied my stomach in knots. "Sounds good."

"And thank you. You've gone above and beyond. You even painted my chicken coop the quirky shade of blue I like."

"You bought the paint. And the chickens don't seem to mind."

She stepped back. "You should go. I don't want your dinner to get cold."

I toyed with the keys, tempted to turn off the engine and join her for goat cheese toast. But I hadn't been invited.

What was wrong with me? Life without women was uncomplicated. Joji was as uncomplicated as a tangle of Christmas lights. I'd do well to remember the reasons I stayed unattached.

"See you in the—tomorrow."

She chewed her lip as she waved.

Looking in the rearview mirror didn't make it easier to leave. Rays from the sinking sun set her red hair ablaze with color. She was like both ends of the magnet—magnetic and repelling.

She stirred an attraction, and with it, she dredged up memories and aches.

When I parked outside the main house, the ranch hands were all walking into the dining hall. Even as hungry as I was, sitting around the table and pretending not to care when they ribbed me about working with Joji held no appeal.

I backed up and turned the truck around. Barbeque was always good.

And at that little place in Stadtburg, I wouldn't be bothered.

After a quick stop by my house to clean up, I headed into town.

The place was crowded, and I had to scan the long picnic-style tables to find a seat. I found a spot at the end of a long table next to a family. "Mind if I sit here?"

The mom smiled. "Not at all. We won't be much longer."

With a tray full of ribs and brisket, I ate, trying to forget about the redhead and all the memories that had surfaced.

The family seated beside me cleared their spot and left.

A redhead, much younger than Joji, hurried up to the table. "Is it okay if we sit here?"

"Sure." I smiled before focusing on my food.

A pillow landed on the bench next to me. "This probably looks silly, but my aunt tangled with a goat and needs a pillow to sit comfortably."

I replayed the words in my head before looking up. "Joji?"

The young redhead slapped a hand over her mouth. "You know her?"

"I've been helping her on the farm."

Her grin stretched from ear to ear. "You must be Clint."

"Yes, ma'am."

"Zach." She waved her hand. "This is Clint, the cowboy who is helping Aunt Joji."

Zach stuck his hand out as he stepped up to the table. "Nice to meet you. I almost feel like I know you."

"That's concerning." I chuckled, hoping they'd take my comment as humorous.

"All—mostly all—good things." He chuckled. "I didn't realize you were meeting us."

"I didn't either. Last I knew she was planning to have her special toast." I fought the urge to look around for Joji.

Zach's brow knitted in confusion.

A hand rested on my shoulder. "I haven't introduced them to my new delight. Right after you left, my niece called and invited me to dinner. So, here I am. Why are you here?" She kept her hand on my shoulder and used it for balance as she swung her legs over the bench and sat down.

"Spur of the moment decision."

"Which sounds completely out of character for you." She nudged my shoulder. "When should I expect a text from Ava asking where you are?"

"Why would she text *you*?" I picked up my tea glass, disappointed that the only thing left in the cup was ice.

Joji shrugged and held out a cup. "Will you get me tea while you're up?"

"Sweet or unsweet?"

"Guess." She tore off paper towels from the stand in the middle of the table.

Serendipity was to thank for this strange coincidence. And if Beau knew I was using words like serendipity, I'd never hear the end of it.

I handed Joji sweet tea.

She sipped it, then smiled. "Perfect."

Flooded with the same thrill as when the teacher singled me out in the third grade, saying my project was the best one ever turned in, I eased back onto the bench beside her. But the reason I knew what to get her tempered that thrill.

Her eyes narrowed. "What made you guess sweet?"

"I prefer unsweet." It was one more way we are different.

After chewing her lip a second, she took another sip of tea. "I guess you've met my niece Haley and her husband Zach." Joji pointed across the table.

"I met them, but I hadn't gotten Haley's name. It's nice to meet you."

Haley grinned. "I can't believe the luck of bumping into you here. I've been wanting to meet you." Her gaze shot to Zach. "What?"

He must have bumped her under the table.

"Let the man eat." Zach offered an apologetic smile. "We've gotten to hear all about the goats."

Conversation continued as we ate, and even when I'd finished my food, I stayed, enjoying the company.

Long after we'd all finished eating, Haley stretched. "I have more photos to edit, so we should probably go."

After we'd piled our trash on the trays, Zach carried them to the trashcan.

When Haley jumped up to refill her tea before leaving, Joji rested a hand on my arm. "They drove out to the farm to pick me up, but they live so close to here. Would you mind taking me home? If it's a bother, then I'll—"

"It's not a bother."

She patted my arm before pulling her hand away. "Thank you."

"Clint, it was great to meet you." Haley smiled. "We worried she was taking on too big a project with that farm, but it sounds like she has a great teacher."

"I'm pretty sure your aunt can do anything she sets her mind to." I stood and held out my arm for Joji to use to get up.

Zach chuckled. "A truer statement I've never heard."

"Thank you for the vote of confidence and the dinner." She tucked her pillow under her arm. "Clint is taking me home."

Short and built like a feather, she didn't give off a small vibe. Authority radiated off her.

People reacted to her the same way the ranch hands

reacted to me. But trying to find ways we were alike wasn't a productive use of my time or brain power.

We walked out to my truck, and as we passed the hood, she tapped a dent. "What happened?"

"Someone was mad at me and took it out on my truck." I helped her in.

"How long have you had this? It's what they call a classic, isn't it?"

"That's a nice way of calling it old. I bought it used thirty-five years ago." I checked my mirrors before backing up.

No one ever asked about the dents in my old truck. No one but Joji.

She snickered. "Someone mad at you? How is that possible?"

That had us both laughing.

The rest of the drive, she stayed quiet, but in a way that didn't feel like she was wrestling back things she wanted to say.

I parked in front of her house. "I'm glad I bumped into y'all."

"Me too." In a quick flash of motion, she leaned across the cab and kissed my cheek. "Night, Clint."

Dumbfounded, I sat there while she slid out. And I didn't leave until after she'd gone into the house.

Using the back gate, I drove home, rubbing my cheek a time or two. Maybe it was good I wasn't going to see her in the morning.

Pulling up to the house, I laughed when I spotted Beau on the porch. I didn't wait for him to start the conversation. "What's up?"

"You missed dinner. Everything okay?"

"Barbeque sounded good. So I drove into town." I pushed open the front door. "Beer?"

"Please."

I grabbed two bottles, and we settled into chairs on the porch.

"They sent you over to check on me?"

Beau popped the top off his bottle using the bottle opener mounted to the porch post. "Lilith and Ava are dying of curiosity. After Ava texted Joji and found out you were at dinner with them, it's all I could do to keep Lilith and Ava off this porch."

"It wasn't planned. They just showed up where I was having dinner."

"I believe you. But that doesn't explain why you skipped dinner without letting anyone know."

"Kind of felt like being alone, but that didn't work out as planned."

"I'm sorry. I didn't think helping her would bother you this much." Beau scrubbed his jaw. "I'll talk to Tyler about helping out at the goat farm. I think he's spent some time around goats."

"I'm fine."

"You aren't fine. Look at you. Anyone can see that skipping dinner isn't a normal thing for you."

"You calling me fat?" I tapped my stomach.

"You know what I mean."

"I didn't skip dinner. I had it somewhere else."

Beau stood and leaned on the porch rail. "Is this because of Scarlett?"

I hadn't heard her name in more years than I could count on both hands. "Not because of her. Just stuff that happened."

"The stuff you won't talk about?"

"Yep."

He dropped back into his chair. "We've been friends since high school. There's nothing you could say that would change that. Why won't you tell me? I don't care if you did something illegal. It's not like I'm going to turn you in."

I laughed and thought about Joji's nephew-in-law. "Joji's niece is married to a Schatz County investigator."

"Then we won't talk about the illegal stuff in front of Joji."

"I didn't do anything illegal. And I still don't want to talk about it." I finished the last of my beer. "Joji doesn't need much more help. In fact, I'm not even going over in the morning. She's handling the chores first thing."

Beau checked his phone. "Crap. My uncle is sending his goats over. I don't want goats."

"How's he doing?"

"He won't ever sell that land, but he's getting rid of the animals a little at a time, so I think he feels worse than he lets on. And he's learning to text on that new phone his son gave him." Beau waved his phone back and forth. "Which is why I'm getting texts from him now."

I picked at the corner of the label on my beer. "I might know someone who will take the goats."

"Trying to sell them will be a hassle." Beau grinned. "Will you ask her?"

"Sure. First thing in the morning."

Now I was adding to Joji's farm for adopted animals. She was going to laugh when I suggested she take in more goats.

CHAPTER 13

JOJI

I woke up to a hungry mama kitty demanding breakfast. But who could blame her? Keeping six kittens well fed was a tough job.

After gently rolling myself out of bed, I stretched. The ache had subsided, but it wasn't gone. Nevertheless, the day awaited, and I was on my own for morning chores.

Mama cat—I really did need to give this cat a name—ran to the kitchen ahead of me, leaving six kittens tumbling over each other in an effort to keep up.

I picked up the smallest, who was getting left behind. "What should I call you?" Maybe a theme would help. With my eyes closed, I tried to clear my head of all thoughts. But then I thought about how Clint's stubble felt against my lips. "I probably shouldn't name you stubble because he'd never come back to the farm once he heard the inspiration for your name."

When I looked away from the kitten, my gaze landed on my purse. The corner of a dollar bill poked out. Inspiration.

"Since you are little, I'm going to call you Peso. And that's Franc, Sterling, Yen, Krona, and the one who thinks he's in charge will be called Dollar. That leaves you, Mama cat. You still need a name."

The sleek black cat flicked the end of her tail.

"I'm working on it. I was helping your baby." I filled her bowl with food, then rinsed out her water bowl and set it on the bathroom counter. I didn't want the little ones falling in. But I set out a lid with water in it, so they could get a little bit of water.

While coffee brewed, I yanked on my boots. Since it was just me, I saw no reason to get out of my comfy pajamas.

With a pail of soapy water in one hand, a mug of coffee in the other, and a pillow tucked under my arm, I tromped out to the barn. "Morning littles, after I feed the chickens and milk your mama, I'll come back and give you milk *and* names. I'm on a roll this morning."

I carried the chicken feed to the pen Clint had built. "Good morning, you beautiful, feathered ladies. Ready for breakfast? Did you leave me any eggs last night?" Expecting eggs so soon would only lead to disappointment. But I'd never been good at curbing my expectations.

I scattered feed, and those five little hens ran around eagerly pecking at breakfast.

"Y'all are going to needs names too." I poked my head into the chicken coop on the slightest chance I'd find something.

Two eggs waited for me.

"Which of you fancy ladies left me such wonderful eggs?"

None of them made any move to take credit.

"That's what I'll call one of you . . . Fancy. And you'll be Nancy. And Pixie. And Trixie." I stared at the only red hen. "And you, my dear, I'll call Scarlett."

With a wave, I left them to their breakfast and delivered the eggs to my kitchen. One of those eggs would be the crowning glory on my goat cheese toast.

Back in the barn, I ran through the rhyme, but getting

everything out was almost second nature. The baby goats bleated for attention . . . and milk.

"Be patient. I have to get the milk first." I locked Maude into the milking stand, then sat on my comfy pillow to milk her. "While we're all here, you can help me name Mama cat. I can't keep calling her that. Or maybe I can. What about Mama Mia?"

The baby goats bleated their approval.

Buying this place had been the right move. I had creatures to talk to, and with my nephews and niece close, I didn't feel completely alone. And I'd made friends to boot.

But talking to animals wasn't the same as talking to people.

"I think that name fits her." Clint strode into the barn.

"Oh, hi! I wasn't . . ." I looked down at my pajamas.

"Expecting company?" He chuckled. "Unicorns, huh?"

"Only on my pajamas for now, but maybe one day, I'll get a couple for out here. They're a bit hard to find though." I wiped down Maude and released her from the stand. "Didn't think I could handle chores all by myself?"

"You don't see me helping, do you?" He shoved his hands in his pockets. "I came over because there's something I need to talk to you about."

Last night.

What had I been thinking kissing that man on the cheek? Now I'd be rewarded with the awkward, trying-to-be-nice conversation where he explained he wasn't interested. He didn't need to say it. That part was clear.

"All right. But listen, last night—"

"It has nothing to do with last night." Every muscle in his body tensed, and that visual wasn't helping.

"Oh, good. I thought you were upset because of that peck on the cheek." I walked Maude out to her pen without turning around.

A more relaxed Clint smiled as I walked back into the barn. "Not at all."

I handed him a bottle. "What's up then?"

Since he was here, he might as well help.

"Interested in acquiring a few more goats?"

The man was a tease.

"I vaguely remember having this conversation." I scooped up the smaller goat and started the bottle feeding.

"Beau's uncle is sending his goats to the ranch, and Beau doesn't want them. I thought maybe you might be interested."

"I'll buy them. Whatever fair price is. You let me know."

"Good. I'll check with Beau and give you a number. And I think we probably need to get you a mule. They are good to have around with goats. Protective. There was one here when we got the place, but he was old."

"And he moved on to the happy farm in the sky?"

Clint nodded, grinning. "Sounds like you've had a busy morning, naming your menagerie."

"These two still need names. Any ideas?"

He glanced down at the goat he was feeding. "He looks like a Pogo. He always looks like he's trying to jump out of the pen."

"Then I'll call this little girl Scooter. Because what kid didn't want a pogo stick and a scooter?"

He shook his head. "The way your brain works."

"I'm just happy it still works. Want to hear the names I chose?"

"You know I do." He finished feeding Pogo.

I followed him out of the pen, and we set to feeding the other goats.

"The kittens are all named after money. Dollar, Sterling, Yen, Franc, Krona, and Peso."

"Peso is the little one?"

"Yes! And the chickens are Fancy, Nancy, Pixie, Trixie, and Scarlett."

The metal scoop clanked as it hit the ground. The color washed out of his face, and Clint headed toward his truck. "I need to run."

"Wait." I hurried after him, feeling horrible for whatever I'd said that dragged in the storm clouds.

He didn't wait. His tires kicked up dust as he drove away.

I was left standing in my unicorn pajamas, wondering what I'd said that stirred up his beehive.

I WALKED into the doughnut shop, choosing to leave my pillow in the truck. After staring far too long at the glass display full of sweets, I chose a chocolate doughnut with sprinkles. It was on my fourth dose of chocolate since Clint had stormed off, but it wasn't helping.

Staying home and moping tempted me, but the yoga teacher had called and wanted to meet. Hopefully, doughnuts would change my outlook.

A tall woman with short brown hair smiled as she stepped inside. "Joji?"

"Yes!" I waved and met her at the counter. "What can I get you? My treat."

"A bear claw and coffee. Lots and lots of coffee."

The lady behind the counter laughed as she handed over a mug. "Refill it as many times as needed. All the fixin's are on the coffee bar."

Remembering my manners, I extended my hand before dropping into my chair. "Thank you for meeting with me."

"I'm excited to hear this idea about goats. I've seen videos, but I've never been around goats."

"I have one or two that won't be invited to our yoga sessions, but all the others are gentle and fun to be around."

For the next half hour, we discussed the possibility of Jasmine teaching yoga once a week out on the farm.

"You're welcome to drive over and meet the goats."

She wadded up her napkin. "I'd love that. Would you be up for a yoga session? We could try it."

I thought of my poor behind. "Sure. What time?"

"Let's say five."

I scribbled down directions, then we parted ways.

One by one, I was marking things off my list. And I needed that focus. Because somewhere on the ranch, Clint was stomping around, and it was something I'd said that had set him off.

CHAPTER 14

I found Beau in the barn, and thankfully, Tyler was there too. "What's going on?"

Beau dragged his fingers through his hair. "The windmill in the south pasture isn't working."

This was a great excuse to avoid going back to Joji's. "I'll take care of it. And, Tyler, if you don't mind helping Miss Sparks with the evening chores. I'm usually there at five."

"Sure. I can do that." Tyler patted one of the horses. "What does she need help with?"

I shifted so that I couldn't see Beau's curious stare. "She's got most of it under control, but she was injured recently. So, she might need you to milk the mama goat and help feed the baby goats."

"No problem."

I turned to face Beau. "I'll take care of the windmill. Let me grab tools, and I'll drive out that way."

"No. I can handle it." Beau headed for the closet.

I laughed but lowered my voice. "You can't. Lilith has banned you from climbing above six feet."

Beau set his jaw. "I don't see her around here."

"Doesn't matter. You're a horrible liar. She'll know. And then you might have to sleep on the couch." I knew exactly which buttons to push.

"Fine, but I'm going out there with you." He grabbed the toolbox. "You're just looking for an excuse to avoid Joji's, and after our talk last night, that has me curious."

"Careful with that. Curiosity killed the cat."

We strode out to my truck. "She asked about the dent in my hood." Maybe if I aired some of what bothered me, it wouldn't bother me as much.

"Did you tell her?"

"Told her someone was mad at me."

Beau slammed his door, then buckled his seatbelt. "That was the night Scarlett thought you'd spent too much time watching the cheerleaders, wasn't it?"

"Don't remind me."

"We were seniors in high school and so stupid."

"I was at least." I drove out toward the broken windmill. "And I appreciate that you've avoided saying I told you so."

He shrugged. "Wouldn't have changed the past."

Being friends so long, he knew when to drop the conversation.

As I climbed up the windmill, hoisting the toolbox with me, Beau shook his head. "Lilith is calling. You okay up there?"

"I'm good. And she knows all. That's what you signed up for."

Beau grinned. "I did. And she does." He waggled a finger at me. "I think you want the same thing."

"Talk to Lilith." I wasn't about to admit that what he had with Lilith made me wish my life had turned out differently and that being around Joji stirred up emotions I thought were long dead.

And I surely didn't need to be thinking about that when I was so far off the ground.

BEFORE PULLING AWAY from the windmill, I checked the time.

Tyler would be showing up at Joji's any minute.

Beau yawned and scrubbed his face. "If you want to drive straight to her place, I'll nap in the truck while you do whatever it is you do over there."

"Tyler can handle it."

"This is where I say something meaningful and deep." He crossed his arms.

I chuckled. "And I'm supposed to wipe away a few tears and then run off to declare my love to a rescued dog. Is that right?"

"I think we saw the same movie. But in all seriousness, if you ever feel like talking, come find me."

"I know. Tomorrow, I'll start working as ranch foreman again."

He nodded. "Goats are being delivered tomorrow."

"I'll make sure they get to her." I stopped next to Beau's truck. "I'll catch you later."

"You are going to miss dinner again, aren't you?"

"Possibly. Not sure yet."

He walked away without lobbing any other questions at me.

My phone lit up with a message.

There is no need to send help. I can handle things. Joji's hurt and fire were both evident in her text.

Sorry I didn't make it over. I was repairing a broken windmill.

I'm guessing Tyler is happy he got to come. I'm not sure he's noticed the goats . . . or the barn. The yoga instructor is here. We were about to do a quick session to see how it works with my goats.

Her response made me laugh. And I could picture Tyler gaping.

I tapped out another text. *You found someone to teach?*

I did. And let's just say she looks better in her leggings than I do in mine. And that is what Tyler noticed.

The mental image of Joji in leggings filled my thoughts, and I imagined her dancing in the barn. Dancing like only I was watching. After scrubbing my face, trying to brush away those thoughts, I texted a reply.

I'll be over there in the morning. Sooner if you need me to drag Tyler home.

Dots danced on the screen.

I waited.

What reply could be taking her so long to type out?

The two-word text that popped up on my screen was like a gut punch.

I'm sorry.

She hadn't done anything wrong. I was the one who'd rudely stomped away in a quiet fit.

Don't be. I'm the one who should apologize.

See you in the morning. Coffee will be ready when you get here.

And toast?

I'll bake a fresh loaf of bread tonight.

I sent a thumbs up and tossed the phone onto the seat.

While working on the windmill, I'd settled on a plan to avoid Joji as much as possible. But that didn't last.

I'd just invited myself to breakfast.

Even though being around her dredged up memories, I relished every minute with her. But it felt selfish soaking up her enchanting energy. I'd never be in a place to return anyone's affections . . . not that she had any for me.

I drove back to my place to clean up a little before dinner and found Kent, one of the other ranch hands, waiting on my porch.

"What's up?"

The guys rarely showed up on my porch. Conversations typically happened at dinner or working somewhere on the ranch.

He lifted the hat off his head and raked his fingers through his hair. "I need to talk to you about something."

"All right." I pushed open the front door. "Come on in."

He followed me inside. "A few years ago, I met this girl."

"And that's when things got complicated, right?" The conversation seemed to be headed in an uncomfortable direction. I could only hope that a bit of humor would slow it down or change the course.

Kent cracked a smile, but concern—or was that pain— filled his eyes. "Yeah."

I sat down. "What's going on?"

He paced next to the table. "After dating for a month, we got married. It seemed like a good idea at the time. I wasn't even twenty. Anyway, we were happy. At least I thought we were . . . until she left. Kissed me goodbye as she walked out the door, saying she'd see me later."

"She never returned?"

"Nope. She called a week or two later and said she'd met someone else." Kent dropped into a chair. "That was five years ago."

I wasn't exactly the person they came to for advice, so whatever he was leading up to had me curious. "I'm sorry. I didn't realize you were divorced."

"I wasn't. We never divorced." He scrubbed his face, then stared at the table for several seconds. "But I got a call earlier today. She died in a car accident."

Why was he telling me? Ava fed them, and often, they'd talk to her when they needed advice or wanted someone to fuss over them. "Kent, I don't know what to say other than I'm sorry."

"And I found out that I have a son. He's four, almost five. She never said a word about the kid. She must've thought the other guy was the father. That's the only explanation I can think of."

"Where is your son?"

Kent's gaze snapped to mine. "Near Houston. I'm leaving for there as soon as we're done. But I came to talk to you because I guess I need to quit. I'm not sure . . . I mean, I need a job, but how can I raise a kid in that small cabin? And what will he do while I'm working? I don't know the first thing about being a dad."

"Kent, here on the ranch, we're family. You know that. There are enough people around here to keep track of one kid. And in the fall, he'll start school." I hoped all of us could manage one kid. "And I think you'll be a great dad. Look at you. You are dropping everything to go meet your son. That's a great start."

Hope sparked in his brown eyes as he dropped into a chair. "Really?"

Nodding, I glanced around, thoughts churning in my head. "How long will you be gone?"

"A week maybe. I'll stay until after the funeral."

"When you get back, you and—what's your son's name?"

"Mason."

"This house is plenty big for the two of you. You can move in here."

Kent shook his head. "I can't ask you to do that."

"You didn't ask. I decided. There are two empty cabins at the bottom of the hill. I'll be fine there."

Kent stood, gripping the edge of his hat. "Thank you. And I'm sorry to leave on such short notice."

"Go meet your son."

"Will you tell the others? I came straight here after getting the call."

"I'll let them know. Keep me posted."

After a handshake, he strode toward the door. "I will. And if you change your mind, I can figure out other housing arrangements."

"I won't change my mind."

Kent left, and I cleaned up. Dinner was the perfect opportunity to give the news, so I'd show up tonight rather than heading into Stadtburg for barbeque.

Was it too much to hope that Ava had invited Joji to join us for taco night?

CHAPTER 15

Wearing my unicorn pajamas, I snuggled on the sofa and gathered the kittens into my lap. A very tired mama cat flopped on the opposite end of the couch, glad for a break.

I tried reading, but my little fuzzies were too much of a distraction. So, I switched to watching TV. After a while, they exhausted themselves and stopped using me as a jungle gym. With kittens asleep in my lap and on my shoulder, I was the picture of an old maid. Single, surrounded by cats, and watching a romance movie was how I'd spend most evenings for the rest of my life.

And it wasn't so bad.

A knock sounded at the door. Maybe Clint stopped in to ask about how Tyler did. Not wanting to disturb the kitties, I sent Clint a text: *Come on in. You have a key.*

His reply wasn't what I expected. *And you have a peephole, but clearly you don't use it. Please check who it is before opening the door.*

I shoveled cats out of my lap and hurried to the door. "Who is it?"

"Ava. I brought pie."

I flipped the lock and opened the door. "Hi. Come on in."

Ava held up a bag. "I also brought taco fixin's. I thought you were coming to dinner."

"I'd planned to, but after yoga, I sat down with Jasmine to plan the sessions."

"Goat yoga?"

"Yep. She'll start next week. Bumpo will not be invited." I put the kettle on the stove and pulled plates out of the cabinet. "I'm getting excited. This place is becoming what I imagined it could be. Once it cools off, I'm going to prep the ground for a spring garden."

"Homegrown tomatoes. There was a place up the road, and they had tomato plants as tall as me. Covered in those little cherry tomatoes."

"Sounds divine. And speaking of, what kind of pie?"

"Lemon chess. I've been making pies for the big shindig this weekend, the grand opening of the venue. You're coming right?"

"First I've heard about it."

"Lilith had an idea about turning part of the ranch into a venue for corporate functions and weddings and such. The rainy winter and Beau's broken leg slowed things down a bit, but it's all ready now. They are throwing a huge party to show it off. Food. Live music. Dancing." She served up two slices of pie as I filled our teacups with hot water. "Be sure to wear your boots."

"Sounds fun."

Ava eyed me over the rim of her teacup. "Why have you been avoiding me? And what's going on with you and Clint?"

"Avoiding you?"

Hoping not to be questioned about my impromptu dinner with Clint, I'd stayed clear of the ranch. That probably counted as avoidance.

"And now you're stalling."

"There's nothing going on between me and Clint." What if he thought there was, and word got back to him that I thought there wasn't? Why was I making it complicated? "And I stayed away because I knew you'd ask."

"If there's nothing going on, why would asking bother you?"

I didn't have a good answer to that question.

My phone rang, and I didn't dismiss the call fast enough to clear Clint's name before Ava saw it.

"Nothing, huh?"

"He's probably calling about the goats that are arriving tomorrow."

She nodded, exaggerating her movement. "I'm sure that's the reason."

The phone rang again, and Ava shook her head. "If you don't answer, he'll show up at your door. Then I'll feel like I need to leave. Please call him. I'd like to stay long enough to finish my pie."

"Fine. I'll call him. And no one is asking you to leave."

She grinned. "Yet."

The phone rang only once before he answered. "Hey."

"Hi. What's up?" I walked down the hall as Ava giggled.

His voice lacked its usual gruffness. "Just making sure you weren't abducted by aliens."

"I'm pretty sure aliens don't knock."

He laughed.

"Ava showed up with pie . . . and questions." I wanted to yank the last word back as soon as I said it.

"Enjoy dessert. I'll be there tomorrow as soon as the goats arrive."

Did that mean he wasn't coming to breakfast?

"Sounds good. I made bread earlier, so it's ready for toast in the morning. Thanks for checking on me."

"Yep." The called ended.

I thumped my head against the wall. Why had I even mentioned that Ava was asking questions?

She crossed her arms as I sat down. All hint of tease was gone from her expression. "I have one question, and honesty would be greatly appreciated."

"What?"

"Are you interested?"

I stared at my pie. "Your brother is—"

She waved her hand. "I don't want diplomacy. You are the only woman he's let get close since Scarlett left. And if you aren't interested, it won't affect our friendship, but I'll gently warn him off."

Scarlett? Now I knew why he'd left and looked like a storm was brewing inside his head. I'd named that stupid chicken the same as his ex.

"Let get close? That isn't exactly how I would describe it." I pictured leaning across the truck and kissing his cheek. "His sentences are usually short. He rarely mentions anything personal. We aren't that close."

"He talks to you. Usually around women he gives nods and grunts. I've known him his whole life."

"I thought he was older."

Ava rolled her eyes. "I've known him *my* whole life. Better? My point is, he cares. And if you don't, he needs to know that."

I picked up the fork, then set it back down. "I care about him. But he's guarded, and hoping seems like a recipe for disappointment."

"I can't promise it's not."

"We're just so different."

She pointed at my plate. "Eat. And haven't you ever heard the saying *opposites attract?*"

I'd heard it, but I'd convinced myself that it only happened in the movies.

∽

BRIGHT AND EARLY, I started the morning chores. Now that I was running the goat farm alone, I saw no need to change the schedule.

I stepped into the chicken pen, and that red hen ran up and started pecking at my ankles.

"Quit. That isn't the way to get what you want. I'll feed you."

She ignored my words and maintained her attack. I felt stupid being chased by a chicken. But once I tossed feed at her, she lost interest in me.

Thankfully, no one was around to witness my embarrassment.

As I worked down my list of chores, hope diminished. Clint wasn't going to show up early.

I walked Maude back to her pen, then dropped feed in the buckets. "Maybe I should paint signs for these pens. What do y'all think?" I latched the pen before heading to the next. "Should I put Guys and Gals or—"

"Billies and Nannies." Clint stood just outside the barn with his hands shoved in his pockets. "Sorry I'm late."

"It's fine. But you did miss me being chased by that annoying red hen. She's started a new habit of pecking at me until she gets what she wants."

"Then she's definitely a Scarlett." He glanced back into the barn. "I'll get the bottles ready."

"Thanks. I'm almost done here."

My conversation with Ava played in my head, and I almost laughed. Did that last bit count as personal information and getting close? Analyzing every word out of his mouth wouldn't help matters. But even if I did, I'd still have lots of free time.

He handed me a bottle, and we each grabbed a kid.

"Have you met Kent?"

"Tall, dark hair?"

Clint chuckled. "That describes most of the ranch hands."

"I think I know who you're talking about. He's quieter than most of the others."

"That's the one. He just found out he's dad to a four-year-old. The ranch will have a little guy running around. That should be interesting."

"He's welcome here anytime. Please pass that on to Kent. I can teach the boy all about goat farming. And as you can attest, that's every child's dream." I laughed, hoping Clint would see the humor in what I'd said.

He stared at the ground. "It wasn't the goats I hated. It was my father."

I forced myself to stay in place, but what I wanted to do was throw my arms around his neck. "I'm sorry."

He shrugged. "He's been dead a long time."

"It's the reminder you don't like."

"Yeah. It's easier to let people think I hate goats." He glanced up as the kid trotted away. "It's not something I talk about."

"Understandable." I stood, telling myself not to grab his hand. "Let's go have breakfast."

He pushed open the barn door. "What kind of pie did Ava bring over?"

"Lemon Chess."

"That's my favorite. Her apple pie is a close second." He slowed his pace to allow my short little legs to keep up.

"I haven't tried her apple pie."

"Grab a slice on Saturday. You won't regret it." He pulled

open my front door to let me enter first. "I'm sorry I painted a target on you."

"I can handle a few questions."

"I don't doubt that." He leaned back against the counter as I pulled out the ingredients for breakfast. "I think you can handle pretty much anything."

Living most of my life alone, I'd heard that comment from more than one person. But never had it meant more.

And that scared me.

CHAPTER 16

*A*fter having a fourth piece of toast and a slice of pie, I finished off my coffee. "That batch of cheese was even better than the last."

Joji grinned. "Thanks."

My phone buzzed, and I checked the message. "Beau texted that the truck is on its way. Should be here in a half hour. I need to go move goats around."

"How long will we need to keep them separate from my goats?"

I scooped up one of the kittens. "Not long, and you may end up getting rid of a couple. The females are good for milking, but the males are really only good for three things—studding, eating, and brush clearing. And wethers are better for everything except the studding."

"Eating?"

"I recommend you don't name those." I studied her expression.

"How many males are we getting?"

We?

I grabbed my hat off the wall hook. "Not sure how many are coming."

She wiped her hands and walked to the door. "Show me what I need to do."

As she stepped through the door, I touched her back. I did it without thinking, but when she stopped and sucked in a breath, I noticed.

Acting like it wasn't an issue meant we wouldn't talk about it. And I definitely didn't want to talk about it. "You really only need one, maybe two billies to use as studs."

"What should I do with the others? I've never eaten goat. And what are wethers?"

I'd been waiting for that question. "Those guys are missing the parts that make them able to stud."

"Ooh." She fell into step beside me, taking two steps for every one of mine.

"We'll have to see what arrives. It depends on what he was using them for. And this whole place is fenced, so you could let some of them wander a bit more if you wanted. After Sutton left, we kept them mostly penned because it made it easier."

"So, the three guys in there . . ." She pointed at Bumpo's pen.

"Bumpo and Boingo are both wethers. Badly behaved wethers."

"Were they intended as meat goats?"

I nodded.

"That's not happening. They can be my lawn service . . . bad manners and all."

I bit back a chuckle. The fire in her gaze amused me. "They're lucky to have you."

"Darn tootin'." She leaned over the fence and hollered at Bumpo. "You hear that? You owe me."

"We'll lock the billy up in one of the stalls and put Bumpo and Boingo with the nannies."

She stepped into the barn and stopped right in front of me. I grabbed her shoulders and tried not to fall on top of her.

Acting as if she didn't notice, she rattled off her question. "If I wanted to get one of those automated milking stations, the kind where I can milk several at one time, where should I put it?"

"I could knock out part of that stall, and it would fit in there." I let go of her shoulders.

She spun around. "I can even pay someone to do it . . . if you don't have time."

Summers on the ranch were busy, so telling her it wasn't an issue would be a complete fabrication. "I'll make time."

Reaching up, she touched her hand to my arm. "Thank you. Not only do I appreciate the help—there is no way I would've learned all this so quickly without your help—but I enjoy having you here. And when we talk."

"You let me know when you're tired of me talking your ear off."

Amusement glittered in her eyes. "More than ten words in one sentence. Don't hurt yourself."

"There's work to be done." I patted her hand that was still resting on my arm. "Goats, remember?"

"Aye, aye, b—Clint." Mischief joined the amusement in her eyes.

I showed her how to ready the stall. Then we moved goats around. We were just closing the pen when the truck and trailer pulled into view.

She grinned and rubbed her hands together. Her dream of expanding the goat farm was becoming reality, and seeing her excited was reward enough for the extra work.

Joji was quick to say she needed me, and I appreciated the

thought. But it was the want and desire flickering in her eyes that interested me more. Sadly, the words that haunted me kept a wall around my heart. I needed to be careful.

Giving Joji the wrong impression would only hurt her. And I'd do anything to avoid that.

I HEFTED the last box into the bed of my truck. "Ava is going to give me grief about how dirty this place is. I'll have to get her something nice for cleaning it all up."

"You don't have to stay in that tiny cabin. We can have another place built."

"First of all, this is a ranch. Not a neighborhood. And I don't need much space."

"But it doesn't feel right having you live in that little thing." Beau pointed down the hill.

"It was good enough for Lilith." I was tired of discussing it.

He shook his head. "Have it your way. But if you ever change your mind . . ."

"You'll be the first to know. I've got this. You need to go get ready for the shindig."

"See you there." He headed for his truck. Before he climbed in, he turned. "You will be there." There was no way to interpret what he'd said as a question.

"Yes, boss."

"Good. Lilith is excited. And that makes me happy."

I understood better than I was willing to let on. "I know."

I hadn't seen Joji in five days, and the distance helped. A little. I still thought about her when I was supposed to be working. And I'd strummed on my guitar more in the last few days than in the last year.

Maybe there was merit to that saying about absence. But

Joji would be there tonight. And Beau had shot down the idea of skipping the festivities.

I drove down the hill and unloaded the last of my stuff. It wasn't as if I had much in the way of stuff, but with all of it stacked in boxes in the small cabin, it looked like a big pile. There was only a narrow path leading to the bedroom and to the kitchenette.

But unpacking would have to wait until later. No one wanted me showing up to a party smelling like I did.

CHAPTER 17

JOJI

Flopped on the bed, I stared at my closet and shifted the phone to my other ear. "Josefina, I'm wondering if I should just stay home tonight."

"No, you shouldn't." She used her mothering tone. "Put on your dancing jeans, and that cute purple top. You know, the one with the ruffles."

That exact outfit was hanging on the doorknob. "He doesn't want to see me. Why did I have to go and open my big mouth?"

"Calm down. It's not like you proposed to the man."

I steered the conversation away from Clint. "I keep waiting for you to propose to Mateo."

She giggled. "We'll see. But I'm going to hang up so that you can get dressed. Call me later."

"I will." I tossed the phone on the bed, then realized I didn't know how to get to the venue. I knew it was on the ranch . . . somewhere. But the ranch was huge.

I shot off a text to Ava. *Will you send me directions?*

I'll send someone to pick you up. She followed her text with a smiley.

Any question about who she planned to send over was answered with that one little emoji.

After a quick shower, I dried my hair and applied makeup. I hadn't broken into my cosmetic bag since buying the farm. Would Clint even recognize me?

Once dressed, I stared at myself in the mirror. No matter what, I planned to have a good time, but I wanted Clint to enjoy his evening. Being there might make it harder for him to do that.

A truck door slammed, and I ran to the door. A deep breath calmed my nerves, and I pulled it open.

"Hiya, Miss Joji. Ava asked me to swing by and give you a ride." Parker flashed his crooked smile.

Clint must've told Ava to send someone else.

"Thank you. Have you been busy getting things ready for tonight?"

"Not so much. They didn't need any horses tonight."

"That's right. You're the wrangler."

"Yes, ma'am." He showed the same courtesy as Clint always did and opened the truck door for me.

"I appreciate the ride. Ava could've just told me how to get there."

"I didn't mind. Most of the other guys were scrambling with last-minute stuff."

Maybe that was why Clint hadn't come. I could pretend, but I knew better. Just like I'd avoided Ava, he was avoiding me.

"It sounds like it'll be a fun night."

"Hope so. But how can you go wrong with live music and dancing?"

"Exactly."

Music wafted over the field as Parker drove under an arched gate. My only goal tonight was to have fun. If I kept reminding myself of that, maybe I'd stop thinking about Clint.

Fat chance.

DAG BOWED after we stepped off the dance floor. "You're quite the dancer."

"It's fun. And with music like this, how could anyone stay still?" I patted his arm. "I'm going to sit this next song out."

He smiled. "And I'm going to see if I can talk that veterinarian into a spin around the dance floor."

"Good luck." I scanned the crowd as I made my way to the dessert counter. Apple pie was calling my name.

I didn't see Clint anywhere. Granted, there were probably two hundred people here, but I'd been looking. When Ava was busy talking to some handsome fella at the other end of the counter, I snuck up and grabbed a plate. Then I strolled out of the big gathering room. People milled about in the open area between the buildings. Laughter and Latin music echoed from the saloon, the smaller of the two spaces.

The tables outside were full, so I slipped inside and found an empty table in the back. In here, the lights were dim. Energy pulsated from the dance floor. Tucked away, I ate my pie.

Clint was right. The apple pie was almost as good as the pie I'd had the other night.

"I'm surprised you aren't in the other building line dancing." Clint nodded at the empty chair next to me. "May I?"

I nudged it to him. "Please."

"So?"

"The pie is really good, and as soon as I finish, I might join in the line dancing fun."

"Lilith knows how to throw a party, doesn't she?"

"For sure."

He scrubbed his face. "I'm surprised to find you sitting in here alone. I mentioned to a couple of the guys that I'd be late and asked them to make sure you were entertained."

"They did. Dag is great on the dance floor, and Parker makes me laugh."

He nodded toward the bar. "Want something to drink?"

"Nah. I think I'm going to go check out the line dancing." Sitting here in the dim light next to Clint with Latin music thumping to the rhythm of my heartbeat wasn't helpful in keeping things simple.

Line dancing was something I could do alone.

As soon as I stood, he was out of his chair. We walked back into the bigger venue, and the band was stepping off the stage.

"Looks like they're taking a break. I should've said something to you sooner." He pointed at the table. "We could sit and listen to the DJ play music."

"Sooner? How long have you been here?"

"Only a little while. Kent got back early, and I was helping him get settled."

Familiar music started, and I grabbed Clint's hand. "Is that the Cotton-Eyed Joe?"

He nodded and stepped back but didn't pull his hand out of mine.

"I've never done it. It looks so fun." I started toward the dance floor.

His fingers slipped out of mine, and I didn't turn around. I watched people's feet as I joined in. I didn't join any of the groups where people had their arms linked.

Being alone offered me the opportunity to learn without tripping up others with my mistakes. Focused on watching my feet, I moved forward, but everyone else moved back.

There were forward steps, back steps, and kicks. I just had to sort out what to do when.

An arm circled my shoulders. "Listen to the music. When this is playing, we move forward." Clint had clearly done this a time or two.

I tucked an arm around his waist and hooked a finger on his belt loop. "Thanks."

Just as I figured out the steps, the music played faster. The faster we danced, the more I laughed.

When the song ended and it switched to the Chicken Dance, Clint tugged me off the dance floor. "That is where I draw the line."

"You dance. What other secrets are you keeping?"

"Plenty. And I intend to keep it that way." If it weren't for his slight grin, it would've come off as gruff.

I ran my fingers through my curls. "Now I think I want something to drink."

"Water, wine, margarita, or Dr Pepper?"

"Surprise me." I pointed to a table in the corner. "I'll grab that table for us."

Us. I shouldn't use words like that. Words like *us* and *we* sent Clint running. And if companionship—and dancing— were all he could offer, I'd learn to be content with that. I had the cats to talk to in the evenings.

He set a margarita in front of me. "Have you talked to Ava or Lilith?"

"No." I sipped my frozen drink. "Lilith looks pretty busy, and Ava—I didn't talk to her."

Avoidance was the reason. I didn't want her giving me a look of pity because Clint hadn't picked me up, and now that we'd danced, I really didn't want to deal with the questions.

"Let me guess. You don't like margaritas?" Why was I intent on pointing out our differences?

"I like them just fine." He lifted a bottle of water. "But I'm driving."

"I've been thinking about your suggestion about selling three of the new billies." In between thoughts of tonight's party, I'd been thinking about the goats. But every time I thought about goats, I thought about Clint. It was wholly inconvenient.

"If you want to keep one of them and sell our billy, that works too. That might be the best solution."

"I can't believe how hard the guy laughed when I asked about names."

Clint chuckled. "He's probably still laughing."

"I think whatever one I keep is going to get named Stud Muffin."

"That poor goat." Clint crossed his arms and leaned on the table. "I'll take care of getting them listed and sold."

"I want to be a part of that process. I need to learn."

He shot me a side glance and nodded. "How have things been? It was a busy week, and I didn't make it over there."

"It's been good. I think I'm past the hand-holding stage." I bumped his shoulder with mine. "But I missed you."

Without looking at me, he smiled. "Let me know the next time you make a loaf of bread. I'll stop in for a visit."

I considered making a fresh loaf every night. "Will do. Oh! This is a good song. Let's dance." I hadn't even noticed when the band went back on stage.

He raised an eyebrow.

"It'll keep me entertained."

"Using my own words against me seems unfair." He stood and held out his hand. "One dance."

Many dances later, he opened the door on his pickup and held out his hand to help me in. "That was fun, but I need to get home. Morning will be here early."

"Chores don't care how much fun we had the night

before." I held my breath when he didn't step away as soon as I was in my seat.

"I did have fun, and I'm sorry I stayed away. I kind of like having more than one friend." He closed the door before I could respond.

I didn't know whether to cry because I'd been relegated to the friend zone or to dance a jig because I'd been included on a very short list.

~

THE COTTON-EYED JOE was still playing in my head when I fed the chickens, tossing seed toward the red hen first so she wouldn't peck at my ankles.

"Scarlett, I think maybe the woman who shares your name did a royal number on my cowboy. And I'm not sure what to do about it." I laughed at myself for talking to a chicken. "Dear advice chicken, how long should I wait before making bread?"

Scarlett continued pecking at the ground, not even bothering to look at me. I'd lost my ever-lovin' mind.

I hurried through the rest of the chores, then studied the new billies as they ate. "It seems downright awful to judge your value based on virility. But I can't keep all of you."

Holding out a chunk of carrot, I waited to see which of the guys would come to me first.

A black and white goat trotted up to the fence, then stood on his hind legs. He thought the carrot treats were better than his regular food.

"Good choice, Stud Muffin. You get to stay. When the time is right, I'll introduce you to the ladies."

Clint would laugh when he learned how'd I'd decided which goat to keep.

Once chores were done, I cleaned up and headed into

town. Talking to animals was a sure sign I needed to be around people, and that doughnut shop in town always seemed to have interesting folks popping in and out.

And maybe I'd see if Haley wanted to grab lunch. She worked right near there.

With a book in my purse and a craving for a bear claw, I walked up to the counter.

"Hello. What can I get you this morning?" The nice woman running the place greeted every customer with a bright smile.

"Good morning. I am in desperate need of a bear claw."

She laughed. "Coming right up. Need anything else with that?"

"Coffee." I swiped my credit card in the little machine. "This is such a cute place. And everything I've tasted was delicious."

"Thank you. I'm glad you like it. It's a lot of work, but I'm loving it." Her eyes shot to the door as a group of firemen walked in.

"They look hungry." I waved as I walked to the table in the corner.

I needed to work this into my weekly routine. Doughnuts two days a week would balance with the yoga one day a week. Balance was important.

*a*fter Lilith's shindig, I expected Joji to message that she'd made bread the very next day. She didn't.

I'd been waiting more than a day.

As soon as this fence was fixed, I'd pop over there to check on the new goats and see how they were settling in. Lying to myself that the goats were the reason had to suffice for now. Any other reason was more than I was willing to admit.

While I was tightening the last wire, Beau drove up. "You done? Our new bull got out, and I could use some help getting him back where he's supposed to be."

"Just finished. I'll follow you." I climbed into my truck and checked my phone for messages. Nothing.

Trying to convince a bull to go where he didn't want to go always took a while. It'd be dinnertime or later before I'd make it over to Joji's.

Beau parked and jumped out. "Tyler should be here with the trailer any minute. I'm thinking I don't like our new bull."

"He's been here a month. This is the third—no, the fourth

time we've had to chase after him. Zero stars. Do not recommend."

"He's just a bit ornery. He'll come around." Beau's smirk and raised eyebrow made his dig clear.

"You calling me ornery?" The label fit me to a tee. Once I made up my mind, I didn't change it . . . unless God shouted from on high. So far, there had been no booming voices from heaven.

"If the boot fits." Beau opened the gate to let Tyler drive into the pasture. "When are you going to tell me what happened with Joji?"

"Nothing to tell."

"I haven't seen you on a dance floor in fifteen years."

"Didn't realize you'd been counting. How *sweet*." I kept one eye on the bull as we walked up to the trailer. "Same plan as last time?"

"Yep. I hope he doesn't remember our tactics."

After a half hour of maneuvering, that bull was probably laughing at us. Or maybe we'd made him mad. Because when Beau moved his arms and tried to steer the bull into the trailer, that beast turned, dropped his head, and headed right toward me.

This was not my day.

If I'd wanted to jump fences and dive away from charging livestock, I'd have become a rodeo clown.

More than likely looking the part, I launched myself over the nearest fence, praying I wouldn't break anything when I connected with the ground. The cracking sound wasn't promising. Neither was the shattering pain that radiated through my foot. I wasn't sure whether to blame the bull or the fence.

But whatever whapped me was going to leave a bruise. I could tell that already.

After rolling away from the fence, I sat up and glared at the ornery fellow, then flashed Beau a thumbs up to let him know I was still alive. That's when my phone buzzed.

It was probably Joji.

I didn't have a chance to check before Beau ran up.

"Anything broken?" He sounded calm, but his eyes told a different story.

I shrugged. "I guess I'll know once I stand up."

"Didn't know you could run that fast." He stuck out his hand.

"Me either." Using his arm, I stood and balanced on my good foot. "You're going to have to call someone else to help you. I'm going to ice this foot and put it up."

"You should see a doctor. It could be broken."

"We'll see."

"Don't be stubborn."

"Look. If it is broken, it'll still be broken tomorrow. And I'll get it checked out then."

"Fine. Let me drive you home. Dag and the other guys can take care of our friend."

I huffed. "Friend. Whatever."

Beau laughed. "He's just out looking for love."

"I'm not sure love is the right word." I tossed Tyler my keys. "Park it by the cabins."

"Yes, sir. Holler if you need anything."

I limped to Beau's truck and climbed in, trying to hide my winces. Anytime I put pressure on my foot, pain stomped on every nerve. I really didn't want a broken bone. I didn't have time for that.

Tyler waved for us to wait, then ran toward the truck.

I put the window down. "What's up?"

"Since you're injured, do you need me to help Miss Sparks? I can go over there as soon as we get the bull where he belongs." He pointed back over his shoulder as if I needed an indication of where the goat farm was.

"Let me guess. She's hosting yoga tonight?"

Tyler grinned. "Rumor has it."

"Sure. She's probably good, but check in with her. And if you need an excuse to hang out there more, she's talked about digging up a spot for a spring garden."

"I'm on it. I'll talk to her about that tonight when I'm there. Thanks!"

Beau laughed as he turned the truck around. "I wonder if Lilith has heard about the yoga. If she has, I might need to go help till the ground for the new garden."

I'd be happy when the love birds moved out of the honeymoon phase of their marriage.

As Beau drove toward my cabin, I slipped my phone out of my pocket. The cracked screen made it a little hard to read the message, but I did see the word *bread*. The good news was that the cracking sound was likely the screen and not my foot.

I tapped out a quick reply, hoping Beau wouldn't ask any questions. *Phone cracked. I'll call later.*

"One of the guys need something?"

"Nope. But my phone fared as well as I did." I showed him the screen.

"Sorry about that. I'll run it into town and get the screen fixed or maybe just get you a new phone."

"I don't need a new phone."

"As foreman, you need to be reachable."

"The phone still works. And I can take care of it. I'll probably be back to normal tomorrow."

"I wouldn't put money on that. I'll be surprised if you can even get your boot off."

"I'll manage." I slid out when he stopped in front of my cabin. "Tell Ava I'll call her later. I don't want her worrying."

"Ava worry?" Beau laughed. "I'll tell her, and she'll be over here with food two minutes after that."

"Tell her to bring an icepack too." I hobbled inside and flopped on the sofa. Sometimes being a cowboy wasn't all that glamorous. Today it hurt.

⁓

"WHAT DID YOU DO?" Ava had one foot inside before she tapped on the door.

I rubbed my eyes, wondering how long I'd been asleep. "I lived thanks to my high jump skills."

"I brought you chicken fried steak and all the sides. Dessert wasn't ready yet." She set a foil-covered plate on the side table next to the sofa. "And here's your ice. Have you taken anything?"

"Not yet."

She disappeared around a stack of boxes. "Give me a second. Have you unpacked them yet?"

"Are trebuchets better than catapults?"

"I don't know." She shook her head. "Just tell me where they are."

"In the cabinet next to the fridge."

She handed me pills. "You still have a sense of humor, so you can't be in that bad a shape."

"I'll be fine. Thanks for bringing me food."

"I'd stay, but I need to get dinner on the table." She looked at my boot. "You should take that off."

I waved her toward the door. "Go. I'm fine. Just don't text me because my phone screen cracked. Texts are hard to read."

"Eat, then go back to sleep. But take that boot off."

"I will. Now, go."

In a fluster, Ava rushed out, and I got my quiet back.

That lasted only a few seconds. When I pulled my boot off, the silence was shattered by my curses.

Even the ice pack caused me pain.

Trying to ignore the throbbing in my foot, I ate my dinner. Then I tilted my head back and closed my eyes. Asleep, I wouldn't be thinking about the pain.

CHAPTER 19

Tyler walked up just as the ladies were putting out their mats. His sense of timing was amazing. "Clint sent me over to check in with you. Need me to do anything?"

"He sent you . . . here?"

"On account of his injured foot. He hurt it in a near miss with an angry bull." Tyler stared over my shoulder a second before remembering I was there. "And he said you might need someone to till the ground for a spring garden."

I'd have to think of some way to thank Clint properly for providing me with a willing laborer. "I do. If you are free on Wednesday night, we could talk about it then. Yoga starts at seven, but we could talk at 6:45. Would that give you enough time for dinner?"

"Yes, ma'am." Tyler tipped his hat. "Sure you don't need me to do anything tonight?"

"Chores are all done. But thanks for stopping by. You can join us for yoga if you'd like."

"Tempting, but I'm pretty sure my jeans won't let me

bend like that." He nodded his head toward Jasmine who looked folded in half.

"I don't bend like that." I patted his arm. "I need to get back over there, but first please tell me, is Clint okay?"

Tyler shrugged. "I think so. But he was limping quite a bit."

"Thanks." I wouldn't be able to concentrate on yoga, but I couldn't just leave.

It would be a long hour.

As soon as the last woman climbed into her car, I ran inside, grabbed the loaf of bread I'd baked earlier that day and some of my newly made goat milk butter, then hoisted myself into my truck. The crate on a rope was the perfect mechanism for getting in and out.

I drove to Ava's, more accurately, to the house next to it.

Showing up at Clint's unannounced rated as one of the worst ideas I'd ever had. This type of thing would send him running for the hills. But right now, he couldn't run anywhere.

And I needed to make sure he was all right.

After three deep breaths, I raised my hand to knock. Clint was probably too sore to even get up. And no one around here locked up their houses. Except me, but I was weird that way.

I knocked as I shoved the door open. "Clint, I brought you a fresh—"

A young boy smiled at me from the sofa. "Hello."

There was an encyclopedia worth of stuff I didn't know about Clint. But a kid?

"Hi, is Clint here?"

He shook his head, slowly and emphatically. "Mr. Clint doesn't live here."

"Mason?" A guy wrapped in a towel ran into the living room, joining our little powwow. "Oh."

I couldn't blame my flaming cheeks on hot flashes. "So sorry. I thought this was Clint's place." I bolted out the door and down the steps.

"Ma'am!"

I glanced back over my shoulder, putting the puzzle pieces into place. "Yes?"

The guy had only his head sticking out the door. "He moved into one of the cabins down the hill. Beau's son lives in one of those other cabins."

I appreciated his subtle hint that I should be cautious before storming into yet another wrong house.

"Thank you. You must be Kent."

Why was I making conversation with the poor man?

His smile was genuine. "Yes. Nice to meet you. Forgive me for not shaking your hand."

"Forgive me for barging in. I really am sorry."

"Think nothing of it." He nodded down the hill. "Best deliver that fresh bread."

I waved, then fanned my face. Going home would be prudent. But when was I ever prudent?

After climbing back into my truck, I drove downhill. How had Clint not mentioned that he moved? And how sweet was Clint that he gave his house to the young dad and his son?

I stopped in front of the cabins and stared like I was on The Price is Right, trying to decide which door to choose.

"May I help you?" A young version of Beau walked up.

"You must be Garret. I'm Joji Sparks." I stuck out my hand to shake his.

He gave it a quick shake. "The goat farm?"

"Yes. That's me. Anyway, I came by to check on Clint."

Garret pointed. "That's his place. The one on the end."

"Thank you."

I stepped up onto Clint's porch and knocked. "Clint, it's me. May I come in?"

"It's probably not locked." Garret motioned for me to open the door. He had no idea what had happened the last time I did that.

But glutton for embarrassment, I pushed open the door. "Hello?"

"Joji?" Clint sounded groggy.

He was trying to rest, and I'd barged in.

"Oh, you're sleeping. I'll come by another time."

"Stay." His command wasn't barked like an order, but the rumble in his voice sent shivers dancing in a conga line up my spine.

I slipped in and closed the door behind me. "I brought bread and butter. I haven't made cheese this week."

He clenched his jaw as he moved his legs. "Come sit."

"You should rest. I was a little worried after Tyler told me what happened. Then you never called, so . . ."

"Tyler talks too much. I'll be fine."

"That watermelon at the end of your leg doesn't look fine to me." I sat down beside him. "Want some now or should I stash this in the kitchen?"

"I'll take some now."

I sprang off the sofa and walked around the boxes into the kitchen. "You should get that looked at."

"If it isn't better in the morning, I will. And watermelon is an exaggeration."

I carried a plate to the couch. "Here you go."

He smiled as he took a bite. "I love your bread."

"I have an idea." Bracing for a negative response, I tried to figure out how to word my suggestion.

"What's that?" Clint reached for a second slice. He inhaled bread like air.

"Come home with me. You don't need to be here alone."

He started to shake his head. "I'll be—"

"I'll bake a fresh loaf and make you the coffee you love."

"Tempting."

In a bold move even for me, I grabbed his hand. "Please let me take care of you. Just this once."

Staring at the empty wall on the other side of the room, he gave no indication that he planned to respond at all.

I waited.

He nodded. "Let me change and toss a few things in a bag."

"I can do that."

"Stay there. I don't need help changing clothes." He hobbled into the bedroom.

"We should probably take your truck. I'm not sure how you'd get into mine."

Laughter echoed from the other room. "That would be a sight. My keys are on the hook by the door."

"I promise to be nice to your truck."

"Much appreciated." He handed me his bag, then draped an arm over my shoulders after picking up his boots. "I'll need these later, and I could use a bit of help getting out there."

"That's why I'm here. To help."

Getting him into the truck was almost as bad as getting him up my porch steps. His pain was obvious, and I wondered if I'd made a mistake asking him to come.

Once I had him settled on the sofa, I mixed ingredients for the bread.

Clint leaned his head back. "Did Tyler stop by?"

"He did. And he volunteered to prep my garden patch." I

walked over and handed him a cup of coffee. "I could kiss you for that."

With the cup held in mid-air, he blinked.

"Don't worry. I won't. I just said *I could*." When I was back in the kitchen, I peeked out toward to sofa.

That coffee cup hadn't moved.

I DIDN'T CHECK on Clint every time I woke up because the poor man needed to sleep. But there was no way anyone could expect me to make it all night without checking on him at least once.

Tiptoeing down the hall, I peeked around for the cats. Mama cat was on my bed, but the kittens had ventured off hours ago.

I stepped into the living room and slapped a hand over my mouth. With his feet propped up on one arm of the sofa, Clint was stretched out on his back, and all the kittens were in a giant knot on his chest.

Even after traveling all over the world, this ranked as one of the wonders. Maybe it didn't rank in the top seven, but definitely in the top ten.

I stayed an extra second, watching the kittens rise and fall as Clint breathed in and out.

Friends. If I pounded that word into my head, maybe this attraction would subside.

I had my doubts.

Satisfied that he'd live through the night, I slid under the covers, burrowed my feet next to Mama Cat, and closed my eyes.

Hours later, I woke up and sprang out of bed. I needed to make Clint coffee before running out to do chores.

Kittens blew past me as I hurried down the hall.

Clint smiled from the sofa and lifted a mug. "Morning."

"You didn't stay off the foot, did you?"

Mischief danced in his eyes. "Would you believe me if I said the cats made coffee?"

"No. They aren't mice, and I'm not Cinderella." I poured myself a cup. "Want breakfast before I head out?"

"I'll get myself some toast. You don't have to wait on me."

I yanked on my boots. "I'm not going to argue with you."

"I like that plan."

As I walked out to the barn, my phone rang. It was early for a phone call from Ava.

"Hello?"

Ava clicked her tongue before saying anything. "I'm shocked. Shocked, I tell you."

Did she know Clint had come over here last night? That sort of shocked me too, but it wasn't like anything had happened.

"About?"

"A few dances and now you're spending the night together." Her tone carried a hint of accusation.

"He slept on my couch. And truth be told, he doesn't really fit."

"Wait! Your couch?" Ava sounded downright confused. "I'm standing outside his cabin and your truck is here. There cannot be two trucks like this in the state . . . or in the world."

"With all his boxes, he would've had a hard time getting around. I invited him to my place, and we came over in his truck."

"You drove his truck?"

"He wasn't in any shape to drive. But he seems a bit better this morning."

"Good to hear. He didn't answer his phone, so I walked over to check on him and found your truck instead. I thought . . ." Ava chuckled. "You know what I thought."

"Your brother loves fresh-baked bread. That's why he agreed to let me fuss over him."

"Not the only reason. I'd love to chat more, but since he's fine, I'm going to the main house to start breakfast."

"Bye, Ava. Could you maybe not mention . . ."

She laughed. "Bye."

Everyone would hear about Clint staying at my place. And he wasn't going to be happy about it.

CHAPTER 20

I blamed my pain haze for agreeing to come to Joji's. But having someone take care of me—someone who wasn't my sister—was a treat I hadn't enjoyed in a long time.

Walking off without my phone wasn't my best moment, but I blamed that on my pain also. I'd call Beau from Joji's phone when chores were done. I intended to spend today on this couch with my foot up.

I slathered butter on my toast, grabbed an icepack, then hobbled back to the sofa. For years I'd said Ava was the best cook in the world. Now I wasn't sure.

Could the company change the flavor of food?

Joji stomped her boots on the porch before stepping inside. "Oh, good. You have ice on it. Your sister called me because you didn't answer your phone."

A shadow crossed her expression, and when she bit her lip, I knew there was part of the story she wasn't telling me.

"What?"

"I told her you seemed better this morning."

"Spill it, Trouble."

Humor lit up her eyes. "She saw my truck and made certain assumptions."

"I didn't really think that one through, did I?" I knew that where I'd stayed last night would be the topic of discussion over breakfast. And it bothered me.

Why couldn't two people spend time together without those around them trying to marry them off? I had no interest in marrying again. But was there anything wrong with enjoying Joji's company?

"I'm still glad you came." Joji dropped onto the floor beside the couch and sipped her coffee.

"Me too." I patted my leg, inviting the kittens to climb up. "I think Peso likes me."

"Seeing you with the kittens all over you was amusing. And sweet."

"I don't need *you* giving me a hard time." I fought the urge to brush my fingers through her hair. "I should probably stay off this foot today. I can show you where to list the goats for sale, and . . . I don't know what else."

"I can make us a peach cobbler, and we can watch a movie. I'll let you choose. Or, if you're craving doughnuts, I can get some from that place in Stadtburg."

I could rationalize my attraction and say that Joji and I were just two lonely people who craved companionship. And that was what I did.

"Sounds good to me. May I borrow your phone to let Beau know that I won't be working today?"

"Sure." She grinned. "I'm surprised he hasn't already called me."

"Right?"

After standing up, she rubbed my arm. "I'm going to clean up and run to get doughnuts. Use my phone as long as you need."

This little home-sweet-home scene had alarm bells firing

in my head. But for the moment, they were being drowned out by the air guitar of excitement.

I dialed Beau and braced for the third degree.

"Hello there."

"Hey. I'm at Joji's, and I'm going to keep my foot up today. The swelling has gone down a lot, but it's still sore."

"Is that it?" He sounded like he was smiling while he talked.

"Unless you have something else you want to talk about."

"Ava and Lilith have a whole list of questions."

Why delay the grilling? "Ask away."

"Seriously?"

"Look. Joji and I are friends. That's all. She offered me her couch, and I got fresh bread and great coffee out of the deal. There really isn't anything to tell." I glanced down the hall, hoping she wasn't eavesdropping. "And today I'm going to walk her through selling some of these billies. She has too many."

Beau was quiet for several beats. "Just let me know if you need anything." The flatness of his tone felt like an accusation, one I deserved. He knew me probably better than anyone else in the world, and he knew my rationalizing when he heard it.

"Thanks. I will."

"And Clint," Beau said as a door closed. "Does she know that it's nothing? Also, I'm taking your phone to get repaired. I don't want to call Joji every time I need to talk to you."

"It's in my cabin."

He hung up without saying another word.

I poured myself another cup of coffee and flipped open one of Joji's photo albums. There were photos from all over the world, and she was alone in almost all of them.

Maybe we weren't so opposite.

That didn't change who I was . . . or wasn't.

When she walked out a few minutes later, I studied her expression a second, hoping to discern whether she'd heard me talking to Beau. If she had, nothing in her face gave it away.

She propped her hands on her hips. "What should we do first? Goats or doughnuts?"

"Let's get the goats listed first. Have you decided which ones to sell?" I shifted to make room for her on the couch.

She dropped down next to me. "I did. I used an incredibly scientific method to evaluate which billy would be the best to keep."

"Did you now? I can't wait to hear how you could tell which billy will sire the best kids."

"Siring had nothing to do with it. I held out treats. The first one to eat the carrot chunk out of my hand earned the name Stud Muffin. I'm keeping the black and white one."

"The goofy-looking one?"

She poked me in the arm. "Be nice to him. I don't want him to get a complex about his looks."

"He's a goat."

"With a Y chromosome." She raised her eyebrows, begging me to counter.

I just shook my head.

"Do you need me to run out and take pictures of the other two goats?"

"We'll need pictures." I watched as she sprang off the couch and picked up her phone.

She stopped outside the door and poked her head inside. "Be right back."

For all Joji's energy, her vivacious smile and enchanting spunk were not enough to drown out the words I'd let play in my head on repeat far too long.

I wasn't even sure how to turn off the tape.

∼

ONCE THE LESSON was over and the goats had been listed, Joji moved her laptop to the counter. "What happens if they don't sell? And don't say we'll eat them."

"You don't want to eat those guys. They'll be too gamey."

"When I was traveling, in one place they served us wild boar. I managed one bite. Nastiest thing I've ever put in my mouth."

"Yep. It's kind of like that. Ask me how I know."

"I'm sorry." She stood in front of the sofa.

I shrugged, trying to give the impression that none of that bothered me anymore. "It was a long time ago."

CHAPTER 21

JOJI

*W*hen shadows of the past darkened Clint's eyes, I knew it was time to give him space. Besides, after hearing him talking to Beau about how Clint and I were just friends, I'd pasted on a smile, and it was starting to slip.

I snatched my purse off the counter. "Doughnut run. What do you want?"

"Surprise me."

That was payback for the times I'd done that to him.

"I'll do my best. No complaining if I get it wrong though."

He laughed as I closed the door.

Once I hit the main road, it was only a few minutes until I parked outside the doughnut shop which was good because I didn't need time to stew about being Clint's friend.

I'd dated some over the years, but no one had tempted me to settle down. Resigned to living alone, I'd settled down, and now my prince charming showed up. The only problem: he didn't think he was a prince. Some redheaded evil witch had cursed him.

If a kiss would undo the curse, I'd line up to volunteer.

That train of thought ended when I parked. Thinking

about kissing Clint was as pointless as dreaming of winning the lottery. And that wasn't going to happen because I hadn't bought a ticket.

I parked my truck far away from the photography studio next door to the doughnut shop. Normally when I was in town, I stopped in to chat with Haley or Nacha.

But today I didn't stop in to say hello. They would ask questions that I didn't want to answer.

I rushed into the doughnut shop and stared at the glass case.

Tessa walked over from a table in the corner. "Hi. What can I get for you?"

"I'm not sure yet. You can visit. This might take me a while." I scanned the shelves, imagining Clint's reaction to each pastry.

She laughed. "Take your time. Just holler when you're ready."

The girl who'd been sitting across from Tessa started talking again. "I love working there, but I need another job and a different place to live. I don't even have a car anymore. What am I going to do?" The blonde dropped her head into her hands.

A lightbulb went off in my head. "I'm sorry for eavesdropping, but—" I stopped when I got to the table and saw who'd been talking.

The poor girl's eyes widened. "You're Haley's aunt. Could you maybe not say anything about me looking for a job? I sort of haven't told them about some of my troubles."

I slid my finger across my sealed lips. "What kind of a job are you wanting?"

Tears brimmed in her eyes. "I'll do anything . . . except be an engineer. I already tried that. Hated it. And I'm no good at fast food. I've tried that too."

"I'm Joji." I stuck out my hand. "And I have a trailer on my goat farm. I could use some help."

Having someone to help with chores and with cheese-making would take my farm to the next level.

Her jaw hung open a second, and I daresay she was questioning what she'd meant by anything. "I'm Cami. And I don't know the first thing about goats. I had a cat once."

"No allergies, I hope. I have several cats. And I'll teach you all you need to know to do the job."

She chewed her lip, then swallowed. "When would I start?"

"Whenever you want." I scrawled my number on a napkin. "And if you want to work parttime at the photography studio, I think that would work out fine."

She bobbed her head. "I'd like that. And I think Haley and Nacha would like that. I've heard them talking about how things are tight now that Nacha is working less because of the baby on the way. You know Nacha, right?" Cami slapped her head. "Duh. She's married to your nephew."

"She is. And we're all excited about the baby." I tapped the napkin. "Call me. I'll bring my truck over and get you moved in. The trailer isn't glamorous, but it's bigger than the little apartment in the back of the studio."

"Thank you." She clapped. "I'm probably crazy for doing this, but it'll be fun, right?"

"Absolutely." I turned to Tessa. "I decided."

"What can I get for you?"

"One of everything you have in the case. I'm pretty sure that'll surprise him."

There had to be a way to undo the curse. Rather than starting with a kiss—his reaction to that comment last night had a hint of horror—I'd take him doughnuts. Maybe Tessa's pastries held a bit of magic.

◞

STANDING outside my house with two bags in each hand, I struggled to open the door.

Before I came up with a solution, Clint saved me the trouble. "What did you buy?"

"Surprise! I bought one of each. You can choose."

He shook his head and reached for the bags. "Just when I think I know what you're going to do, I'm wrong."

"What did you *think* I was going to bring you?"

"We'll never be able to eat all of these." His avoidance of my question made it clear he wasn't going to answer.

I set the boxes on the counter and opened every lid. "I'll give the rest of them to the ranch hands."

"And they'll love you forever."

They weren't the ones I wanted to love me.

Clint picked up a chocolate sour cream doughnut, then sat down at the table. "So, um, I heard something about you walking into the wrong house."

I waved an éclair at him. "*Someone* didn't mention that they'd given up their home and moved into a tiny cabin." I broke my éclair in half and licked the cream out of the center. "I can't believe he told on me."

"It was Mason who told everyone at dinner about the nice lady with the bread."

"He didn't mention anything about the shower and the towel, did he?"

Clint choked on a bite of his doughnut. "The what?"

"Forget I said anything. If you don't see me around the ranch for a while, you'll know why."

After staring at me half a second, he chuckled.

He probably thought I was just trying to make him laugh, and I was content to let him think that.

The kittens chased each other up the hall, and Clint

watched them. "I know how you like to rescue creatures and bring them home. My friend found an old dog on the side of the road. It needs a home, but Blue, Beau's dog, isn't keen on sharing the ranch."

I knew how this story ended. "When are they bringing him over?"

"Tomorrow." He raised an eyebrow. "Is that okay?"

"Sure. I guess that's what I get for leaving you my phone." I walked into the kitchen and made coffee. "Speaking of bringing things home . . ."

"Uh-oh."

"Someone will be moving into the trailer soon."

"What do you know about this person? Are you sure you can trust them?" He hobbled into the kitchen. "Have you asked Haley's husband to check them out?"

Clint's reaction surprised me. I hadn't expected him to be so protective. I didn't really mind. Much.

"I'm pretty sure Haley doesn't want Zach checking out other women."

Clint rolled his eyes, which was a rare treat. "You know what I mean. You can't just invite strangers to live out here. It's not safe."

"I know Cami. She works for Haley, but she needs more employment and a place to live. I can offer her both." I made a display of looking down at his foot. "I thought you were going to stay off it."

"It hardly even hurts." He wasn't being completely honest based on the tightness in his jaw as he put pressure on his foot. "I'm planning to work tomorrow." He poked through the boxes and picked up a lemon-filled doughnut. "But today you promised me a movie. What are we watching?"

"You were supposed to choose."

"Die Hard."

"Sure, then afterwards we can sing Christmas carols." I handed him a mug of coffee.

"Did I mention that you might want to get a mule? They are good for protecting the goats."

"So are llamas." I sat down at the other end of the couch, leaving a reminder gap. I needed the visible reminder that Clint and I were just friends.

For now. I hadn't given up hope that things would change.

Clint shook his head. "Out here, most people just get a mule."

I flashed my sweetest smile, which was easy after downing all that sugar. "Clint Jackson, *I* am not most people."

Whatever thoughts ran through his brain did not leave his mouth. His ability to remain silent had probably served him well. It was a skill I didn't have. And I saw no point in trying to learn it now.

But maybe I hadn't given myself enough credit. I'd managed to go all day without telling Clint I'd heard his conversation with Beau. And it wasn't for lack of thinking about it.

When the movie ended, I threaded my fingers through my hair. "What are you hungry for? I'll make us dinner."

He grabbed his boots. "I should probably go." After wincing as he yanked on his boots, he grabbed his bag and walked out the door.

There was no extended goodbye. Actually, there was no goodbye at all.

I sank onto the couch. The day had started much better than it had ended. Suggesting dinner sent him running. I did not understand that man.

But I had other things to worry about. I grabbed a bucket and cleaning supplies, then headed to the trailer. I wanted it to sparkle for Cami.

CHAPTER 22

CLINT

*W*hen Joji had offered to make dinner, the panic that flooded over me was crippling. The house was instantly too small, and I needed space.

It wasn't until her truck came into view that I remembered important details like not saying goodbye or thank you. Or getting Joji her truck back.

Instead of parking, I turned my truck around.

Back at the farm, I knocked at her door. She didn't answer, so I pushed open the door a little. "Joji, you around?"

I received a couple of meows in response.

Where could she be? It wasn't like she could drive anywhere. Or maybe she'd taken her car. Trying to ignore the pain, I walked to the garage.

Inside, her classic Mustang was parked in its usual spot.

Maybe she was venting to the goats about my bad behavior. I hobbled out to the barn, figuring I'd find her there.

But Joji wasn't in the barn.

Panic was back, but this was a completely different variety.

Asking the goats where she was would serve no purpose, but I did it anyway. "Stud, do you know where she is?"

Her chosen billy stood up and stuck his head through the fence, probably hoping I'd feed him carrots.

"I don't have any treats." When I didn't get any answers from the goats, I walked back toward the house.

Standing next to my truck, I turned in a circle, hoping to spot a clue to her whereabouts. I squeezed my eyes closed and laced my fingers together, resting them on top of my head. She had to be somewhere.

The song "Born to Be Wild" carried on the breeze, and I chased the sound. When I opened the door of the trailer, I was shocked that the walls weren't pulsating.

Checking one room at a time, I searched for Joji. In a back bedroom, a big speaker was right next to feet sticking out from under the bed.

"Hey there."

A thunk and curse word sounded from her hidey hole. Surprising her had been a poor choice.

She slid out and sat up, rubbing her head. "Hey."

"I'm sorry for leaving in a rush."

Her quick shrug didn't make me feel any better.

"Do you want to ride with me to your truck? And what were you doing under the bed?"

"Cleaning. What do you know about this bed?"

I understood her jump in topics as well as I could read ancient Greek. "Zilch."

She scrunched her mouth into a thoughtful pout. "I'm going to assume she bought it new and that it isn't where her husband died."

"He died in the barn." I'd heard about the poor man's heart attack.

Her face paled a shade. "You might've mentioned that before."

"I'm sorry. I didn't get that memo." I glanced around the trailer. "If you're busy, I can come back later and give you a ride to your truck."

"Nah. I just started. I'll come back in here once I get back." She brushed past me and headed out the door.

"Joji."

She stopped on the top step and slowly turned to face me. "Yes?"

"Thank you. For everything."

"Anytime." She took another step down, then turned again. "Please don't make it sound like a goodbye. I enjoyed this." She moved her hand back and forth as she looked up at me.

With her partway down the steps, the height difference between us was now comically exaggerated. I walked down the stairs and stopped at the bottom. "I did too, but I didn't want . . ." How was I supposed to finish that sentence?

She crossed her arms. "You didn't want me to get the wrong impression."

Nodding, I dropped my gaze to the ground. "I'm sorry."

Rubbing my arm, she smiled as she walked past me. "Let me grab my keys."

All my life, I'd kept my circle small. I liked it that way. And how this petite redhead crashed into that circle so quickly still had me dumbfounded. But having her accept what I could give with a smile cemented her spot in that circle.

I limped back toward my truck, tired of my foot hurting. The pain had eased, but it wasn't gone. And after sitting most of the day, that didn't seem at all fair.

She opened the door, piled boxes of doughnuts on the seat, then climbed in. "Thanks for coming back. I would've remembered my truck when I needed it. And I definitely don't need to spend the night with all these doughnuts. Bad idea."

"I'll take them to the dining hall."

Comfortable silence filled the cab as we drove.

When I parked next to her truck, she reached over and patted my arm. "And you don't have to be sorry. But if I ever meet that redhead, hold me back." Laughing, she slid out of the truck and waved after slamming the door.

Joji was like a small flaming cocktail. Compact with an immense amount of energy.

I'd be crazy not to want her in my circle.

Beau must've been watching the cabin because only minutes after I settled on my couch, he knocked as he pushed the door open. "You decent?"

"Don't you think you should ask that *before* you open the door?"

He shrugged. "You seem in good spirits. Where's Joji?" He laid my phone on the table. "Screen was an easy fix."

"She's at her house, and in answer to your earlier question, yes. She knows we are friends."

Scratching his head, he dropped into a chair. "Does she hate you now?"

"No, we're friends."

"I assumed those 'we're just friends' conversations always ended badly."

"You and me both. But Joji is different." I tucked the phone in my pocket.

Beau stood, a smirk dancing on his lips. "Different? We'll go with that."

"She is. I've never met anyone like her. I've been mostly clear about my intentions, and she seems fine with that. But we don't need everyone acting like . . . like I don't know what."

He scrubbed his chin and didn't say whatever was

churning inside his brain. "You coming to dinner or should I bring you a plate?"

"I'll be there. I need to shower first." I grabbed the boxes of sweets. "Take this over to the main house, will you?"

He peeked inside the top box and smiled. "Sure. How's the foot?"

"It's better. I'll be back working tomorrow."

"Light duty." He set his hat on his head. "See you in a bit."

I'd take whatever duty he'd let me do. Joji had sufficiently distracted me for one day, but sitting around too long would make me crazy.

IT WAS NEARLY eight in the evening, and I hadn't talked to Joji since I dropped her off at her truck yesterday. But the dog had arrived, and I headed over to deliver her new rescue.

"You're going to like her. She'll probably spoil you a little, and if you're nice to the cats, she might let you inside."

The chocolate lab cocked his head.

"And she'll give you a name. It might be crazy but pretend like you like it. We don't want to hurt her feelings."

I parked close to the house.

Tyler was on the side of the house, attacking the ground with a tiller, and surprisingly, he was wearing a shirt.

Joji and company were in the fenced field next to the goat pen, doing some bridge thing on their yoga mats. Standing on the porch, I watched. The dog sniffed the entire porch and door, then lay down at my feet.

It was good Joji was getting a dog out here. The chickens weren't going to alert her to danger.

Joji waved as the women folded up their mats.

"That's her. The cute one with the red curls." I nudged the dog as Joji made her way to the porch.

She grinned and stopped next to me. "Do we know his name?"

"Nope. No tags."

"Have you run down a list?" Squatting, she rubbed his head.

"Of dog names?"

"Yeah. You know, saying the name and seeing if he responds. Fido, Butch, Pedro."

The dog didn't even pick up his head.

This was going to take hours.

"Why don't you just give him a name?" To me, that seemed like a completely rational idea.

Joji shook her head. "He has a name. I just need to discover it." Studying the dog, she cocked her head. "What would someone name you?"

"I guess I'll leave you to discover his name."

"Or you could come in and have some peach cobbler. I made some earlier today." She pushed open the front door. "And you can come in too if you won't chase the cats."

The dog stood and sauntered into the house as if he understood every word.

I hung my hat on the hook near the door. "How are you built like that? You eat like I do."

She grinned. "Fast metabolism."

Within minutes, I was seated at the table with a warm bowl of cobbler.

Joji pointed at the dog. "I like him already. Look at that."

Sprawled on the floor, the dog looked up as kittens crawled all over him. Mama Cat stood on the other side of the room, cautiously watching.

"Chocolate . . . Cocoa . . . Brownie." Joji was not giving up her quest to discover the name any time soon.

I devoured the cobbler, then pushed my bowl toward the

center of the table. "I should probably go. I still need to unpack some boxes. Did you finish in the trailer?"

"I did. And Cami called me today. I'm picking her up tomorrow. That place has good bones—"

The dog barked and wagged his tail.

"What do you hear, boy?" Joji stood and looked out the window. "Anyway, like I said. It's not fancy, but it has good bones. I hope she likes it."

The dog stood, scattering kittens on the floor, and walked up to Joji, his tail thumping the leg of the chair.

She stared down at him. "What's got you excited?" Her eyes widened. "Are you Bones?"

Bones answered with a quick bark and more wagging.

"Well, Bones, it's nice to meet you." Joji stuck her hand out, and Bones laid his paw in her hand. "You're a doll."

"Do you need me to make a store run to get dogfood?" I couldn't believe she'd figured out the dog's name.

"Already have some." She patted Bones, then walked into the kitchen. "But you have to eat on the porch. The kittens would never stay out of your bowl." She poured food into one stainless steel bowl and filled the other with water. "Will you grab the door?"

I jumped up to open it. "I'll feel better knowing that you have a dog around."

She set the bowls down which made Bones quite happy. "I feel safe out here. I know there are dangers, but it's quiet. I like it."

My phone buzzed, and I yanked it out of my back pocket. "That stupid bull is out again. He's trouble."

"Don't call him that!" Joji propped her fists on her hips. "That's my nickname, and I don't intend to share it with a bull."

"Yes, ma'am. Call me if you need anything. I'm going to

supervise the other guys getting Houdini back where he belongs."

Joji clutched my arm. "You named him."

"He earned it. If he'd broken my foot, I might've named him Steak." I tipped my hat to her before walking down the steps.

"Please be careful."

"I plan on it."

She stood on the porch, talking to the dog as I drove away.

I liked where this friendship had landed. And I might need to find reasons to work near the barn on yoga days. Those reasons had less to do with the friendship and more to do with how Joji looked in leggings.

CHAPTER 23

JOJI

*W*hen Cami and her boyfriend Harper parked outside the trailer, I ran out to greet them.

Cami seemed both appreciative and horrified. "This looks rugged enough that I might expect cowboys to go riding by. Not that I'm in the market or anything." She twisted her fingers. "I can't thank you enough."

"You are very welcome. The guys should be here soon." I motioned her toward the trailer. "I'm guessing you want to see inside."

Cami walked up the steps. "Is it open?"

"It's open. I don't lock much around here. Anymore. But I have keys if you prefer to keep it locked."

"Yeah, I'm not used to the small-town camaraderie of letting anyone just walk into your house." She grabbed Harper's hand.

"It took me a little while to get adjusted. As far as what you'll drive, I'll give you the keys to my truck. Think you can drive it?"

Her gaze cut to my purple goddess, and her head bobbed

slightly, which didn't give me a surge of assurance. "I'm sure I can."

"You can drive it around here to get the feel of it. It's a bit big for me."

She laughed. "The milk crate gives that away."

Harper grinned. "It's hard to picture Cami driving it, but I'm sure she can handle it."

"Let's go in and look around. I'll show you the rest of the farm after the guys unload stuff." I was excited about having someone else on the farm.

"Great." She turned the knob.

The door swung open without even a creak thanks to Clint and his can of spray. He'd attacked anything with a squeak a couple of weeks ago, then he'd come back after finding me in the trailer because that door made a noise.

Clint was both handsome and handy.

Cami walked through the trailer, dragging Harper behind her.

I followed them, giving the couple a bit of space. "It's not huge, but there is a decent-sized kitchen, two bedrooms, two bathrooms, and a living room."

"I can't cook, so the kitchen is great. Plenty of room for frozen dinners and snacks. I think it's wonderful." Her smile seemed a tad forced.

"Not what you're used to, is it?" It wasn't hard to guess that she'd come from money.

She shook her head. "But it's way better than the tiny efficiency at the back of the studio. Haley and Nacha were thrilled with me switching back to part time."

"I'm glad it all worked out. Later, I'll introduce you to the animals. There will be a quiz on their names tomorrow."

Her brow pinched. "That's a joke, right? Please say it is."

It was going to be fun having Cami around.

As we stepped out of the trailer, Clint pulled up.

When Parker, Tyler, and Dag piled out of the pickup, Cami slipped her arm around Harper's waist. "Aren't you glad you came to help?"

Harper laughed. "Better believe it. I'm not sure I like this new arrangement."

"You don't trust me?" Cami poked him in the side.

He shot a glance toward me. "That's a trap, right?"

I nodded and walked out to greet the guys. "Thank you so much for coming. There are brownies baking for after."

Clint strolled up. "Why do you think I came?"

"How's your foot?"

"Tender but tolerable. I best go supervise . . . unless that's your job."

I patted his chest, a reach worth the effort. "Have at it. I'll tend to the goodies."

While the guys worked, I stayed on the porch, running in to check the brownies from time to time. Cami had her hands in her hair, looking slightly panicked.

There weren't as many boxes as I expected, and even less in the way of furniture. That worked perfectly because the trailer had the basic pieces. It just meant I didn't have to store them somewhere.

After a quick check on the chocolate goodies, I ran back out to the porch.

"It's almost as good as a sitcom." Clint sat on the top step.

I dropped down next to him. "Yep. This would have taken us a lot longer without the help, so thank you."

"Tyler keeps looking around." Clint bumped my shoulder. "Think he's hoping Jasmine shows up?"

"I think you're right." I twisted to look at him. "Cami needs something to drive, so I'm going to let her use the purple goddess for a while."

"Let me know when she leaves the house so I can stay off the roads." He winked.

"I'm going to need something to drive. Any chance you'll help me choose a more suitable truck?"

"Trouble, that purple goddess suits you pretty well . . . if you ignore the fact that you need a crate on a rope to get in and out. Yes, I'll help you."

"I'm thinking blue. I like blue."

Clint rested his arms on his knees and stared at the guys hauling in the last of the boxes. "You could get flames painted on the side."

"That's a good idea." I used the railing to get up. "Come help me serve dessert."

"Yes, ma'am." He shook his head. "Before I met you, only Beau gave me orders."

"How boring. Aren't you glad I showed up?" At first, I didn't turn around to see his reaction, but when he hadn't said anything after a few seconds, I spun to face him.

He grinned. "Very glad."

Dang it. Why did he have to be so charming and so unavailable?

I still hadn't ascertained if a kiss would break the curse. But trying that would scare him off, and that was the last thing I wanted to do.

Laughter snapped me out of my musing, and I stuck my head out the door. "Come on in. I'm serving the brownies now."

Clint moved to the other side of the room, typical behavior when we were around other people.

But just like every other recent visit, his hat was hanging on my wall.

He felt at home here. And that detail mattered to me.

∾

CLINT KICKED the tires of the blue pickup that had no lift and side steps that folded out when I wasn't driving. "Get in. Make sure"—he paused, letting his gaze sweep over me—"that you like it."

I shook my head as he opened the door. "You were going to say *Make sure I can get in,* weren't you?"

"But I didn't." He chuckled. "Hop in."

Grabbing the steering wheel, I hoisted myself into the seat. It was much easier than using the crate. "I like it."

The salesman grinned. "I'll draw up the paperwork." He hurried toward the building.

Clint hung back, accustomed to my pace. "It's pizza night at the ranch. What do you say we grab barbeque at that place in town?"

"What's Ava doing?"

"She's prepping food for a wedding. I don't know the details. It has something to do with the venue." He pulled open the door to the showroom.

"You don't like pizza?" I wanted to know these things about him.

"I like barbeque better. Any more questions before I get an answer?" He stopped outside the office where the salesman was typing away at a computer.

I squinted one eye like I had to think about my answer. Then I patted his chest. "Sure. What are your feelings on barbeque pizza?"

He shook his head. "Never had it."

A half hour later, I drove off the lot in my shiny new truck, then drove the two minutes down the road to the barbeque place.

I parked outside the restaurant, and Clint parked beside me.

Instead of jumping out, I made sure I had everything. My purse. My keys. My phone.

He rapped at the window before opening my door. "You ever getting out?"

"I was waiting on you to open it. That door is so heavy and hard to work." I slid out, missing the side step altogether.

Rolling his eyes, he closed the door. "Sometimes I have no idea if you're being serious or not."

Laughing, I stepped inside after he pulled open the door. The aroma of smoked meat met me.

He set a tray on the counter then motioned for me to go ahead of him. "Figured there was no point in getting two trays."

I ordered what I wanted, overestimating how much I'd eat. When we got to the cashier, I opened my purse, then stifled a gasp when his hand landed gently on mine.

"I've got this. We're celebrating your new toy."

"Thanks." Swallowing back surprise and whatever feeling that accompanied it, I smiled, hoping he couldn't hear my heart pounding.

His touch was infrequent, but every time we made contact, my nerves danced a jig. But because it was obviously one-sided, I worked to wrangle my expression . . . and my feelings.

Evenings spent with Ava and Lilith filled my head with hope because Clint wasn't like this with other people. By people, they meant women. Chats with my friend Josefina kept me more grounded. If he could only offer friendship, was that enough?

Two weeks ago, I'd have answered with a resounding yes, but now? The answer wasn't as clear. I liked him. But I liked him too much.

We sat at the end of a long table, and I couldn't even tell you who sat next to us during dinner. At the end of the evening after laughing and joking, my heart ached.

I felt this way after every glorious evening. Tonight was no different.

He set his pace to mine as we walked back out to our trucks. I hated the small voice in my head that whispered, *"Maybe tonight will be different."*

It wouldn't be different.

"Be careful going home. We might be getting some weather later this week, so . . ."

"Do I need to do something to prepare?" Since I'd gotten to the farm, we'd had rain, but I hadn't dealt with any big storms. And I knew Texas storms could be scary. I stopped with my back to the truck, looking up and waiting for a response.

He stepped closer. "Probably nothing to worry about. I'll come by and check fences if I can get away tomorrow."

"Clint, you have a ranch to run. Just tell me what to do."

"Make sure the fences are secure. When the storm is headed this way, close up the chicken coop and the barn."

"Will the goats be okay outside in their shelter?"

He nodded. "They should be fine. They have a place to get out of the rain. But if you need me . . ."

Oh, I needed him, but two seconds after those words left my mouth, his taillights would be disappearing around the corner.

"I know where to find you." I turned to get into the truck at the same time he reached for the door handle. We ended up tangled. "Sorry."

He rubbed the back of his neck. "Yeah. I was just . . . gonna open your door."

Even the thoughts in my head were making the night awkward. I stepped aside and waited while he opened my door.

Once I was in my seat, he closed me in. That saved me from spilling feelings that didn't need to be said.

All the way home, I lectured myself on how I should behave around Clint. I had a surprisingly good handle on my actions. My thoughts not so much.

When I parked, Cami ran out of the trailer, her face pale. "Help me, please."

"What's wrong?" I jumped out of the truck and ran over. "What happened?"

"I fed the goats just like you taught me."

My heartbeats paused, and I held my breath, waiting for the next words out of her mouth. I was almost afraid of what might've happened to my goats.

She yanked at the ends of her hair. "The brown one jumped out of the pen, and now I can't get him out of my trailer. He's eating my favorite pillow!"

Holding back laughter, I ran into the trailer. "Boingo!" I didn't need her to describe which one it was. Only one of my goats jumped fences. Unless he'd been giving lessons in bad habits to the other goats.

The goat cocked his head, the pillow dangling out of his mouth.

I pointed outside. "Get out there. Leave her alone."

He went right back to chewing.

"I'll be right back." I ran to the barn and picked up the leash—I think Clint called it something else—that I used when I needed the goat to go where he didn't want to go.

When I made it back to the trailer, I moved toward Boingo. "Hey there, sweet boy. Let me get this on you." From a foot away, I launched at him, and after a few seconds of wrestling, I managed to get the leash on his neck. After more sweet talk and lots of cajoling, Boingo was back in his pen.

We'd see how long that lasted.

"He really likes you." I dusted off my jeans.

Cami huffed. "The feeling is not mutual."

"I'm sorry about your pillow."

She shrugged. "I'll get over it. It was the only thing worth keeping from my ex. He was horrid, but he had a great personal shopper." She stuck her hands into the pockets of her overalls, which she managed to make look like something off a runway. "Thanks for getting him out."

"No problem. Have you had dinner?"

She shook her head.

"Come on in. I'll make you something."

She smiled. "I like your new truck."

"Have you driven the other one yet?"

Her lips pinched. "I sit in it at least once a day. I'm working my way up to driving it."

"You've lived here two weeks."

"I'm kidding. Yes, I drive it. And I actually kind of like it."

"I thought you might." The purple goddess had a way of making people feel powerful.

Cami and I were halfway through a movie and more than halfway through our second bowl of popcorn when Bones lifted his head and barked.

Her eyes widened. "Who do you think it is? Should you grab a bat or something before going outside to see why he barked?"

"Calm down." I made my way to the door, and Bones ambled along beside me, his tail wagging. "You're giving me mixed signals, Bones."

"Trouble. You okay?" Clint sounded worried.

I opened the door. "I'm fine. What's up?"

He stepped into the house and inhaled. "You haven't answered any of my messages or calls."

I patted my back pocket. "Dang it. I must've left my stuff in the truck."

Shaking his head, we walked outside. He returned a second later holding my purse and phone. "Here. I need to get Boingo out of the bed of your truck. I swear I don't know what has gotten into that goat. He used to just climb trees."

"I think he has a crush on Cami."

Cami giggled, and Clint's gaze snapped to the couch.

"I didn't know you had company. I'll see you later."

I followed him out to the porch. "Is something wrong?"

"Nope." He kept walking.

I ran down the steps and stopped when I stepped onto the rocky ground. "Ouch."

He whirled around.

I moved back onto the bottom step. "Don't be that way. We aren't high schoolers. What's wrong?"

"I messaged telling you to make sure the windows in the chicken coop were all closed when it stormed, but you didn't answer." He shifted, kicking at a clump of weeds. "I'm not used to worrying about people. And I don't like it." Not once did he look up.

I sat down on the step. "It's nice having someone looking out for me."

"I need to get that fool goat back where he belongs." His shoulders slumped, he strode toward the barn.

It seemed to me I wasn't the only one being tortured by our friendship.

CHAPTER 24

*R*acing to get everything in order before the storm hit, Parker made his way down one side of the barn, making sure all windows and doors were closed and latched. I did the same on the opposite side of the large building.

Pausing, I slipped my phone out of my pocket and checked the radar. "Red bands will be here soon. I'd rather you be home when they hit."

"You and me both." Parker moved from one stall into the next.

I worked quickly, wanting to get to Joji's before the storm arrived. I hadn't spoken to or texted her since I'd made a fool of myself earlier in the week. That whole part about me worrying hadn't changed. And now, what was supposed to be a bad storm was predicted to be a monster. My worry was growing by the minute.

Kent hurried into the barn with Mason in tow. "Dag needs help getting one of the cows back into the pasture. The storm has it spooked. Parker, can Mason stay here with you?"

"Sure thing!"

I waved. "Hey, little buddy."

Relief washed over Kent's face. "Thanks! How long will you be here?"

Parker peeked out of a stall. "Not sure, but I'll meet you at your place."

"Sounds good." Kent patted Mason's head. "You stay with Parker and Mr. Clint, okay?"

Mason nodded. The kid was adjusting well to his new life. In one sense, a four-year-old living on a working ranch was like landing in the pages of an adventure novel. But Kent deserved credit too. He was proving to be a great dad.

I hoped explaining what we were doing would help Mason not be scared. "We're trying to get the ranch ready for the bad weather. The horses and cows don't like the storms."

Mason shook his head. "I don't either."

Parker walked out of the last stall. "I'm just about done. Mason, why don't you run out to my truck? I'll be out in just a second." After motioning toward the door, Parker ran back to the tack room.

Mason stared at the ground.

"The rain hasn't started yet. You'll be okay." I opened the door and stood in the opening. "I'll watch you."

With a brave face on, Mason marched outside.

As promised, I watched as he walked toward Parker's truck.

A crash behind me warned that tonight wasn't going to be good. "You okay?" I waved at Mason, then ran to check on Parker.

He walked out of the closet. "I'm fine. You go. I'll only be another second."

"Don't leave that kid too long. He doesn't like the storm." Thunder rumbled, urging me to hurry to Joji's. "If you need me, call. I won't be gone long." I hadn't told anyone where I was headed, but my guess was that they all knew and politely didn't say anything about it. At least to me. I could only imagine what they were saying to each other.

But right now, I didn't care.

I climbed into the truck and tore away from the barn. My rain poncho was piled in the passenger seat, and I was glad I'd thought to grab it. Because I had it, maybe I wouldn't need it.

Fighting the wind, I struggled to keep the truck on the road. This was only the beginning. The worst was still to come.

Driving faster than was safe for roads out here at night, I made it to Joji's in record time. Rain drops splattered on my windshield, and I jumped out as soon as I'd cut the engine.

I was two steps toward the house when I heard Bones barking outside the barn. Running through the rain, I swallowed back the uneasy feeling in my gut. Thunder rumbled again. Why was Bones outside?

Joji must be in the barn. Why wasn't she in the house?

"Trouble, where are you?" Hollering was pointless because I could barely hear myself over the pounding rain.

Bones ran past me and stopped at the back door that led out to the other pens.

"Is she out there with those stupid goats?" I hurried out, wiping rain out of my eyes. Too bad I hadn't grabbed my rain poncho off the seat.

The free-standing shelter in the goat pen was on its side, and Joji was yanking on it.

"What are you doing?" I grabbed her arm, tugging her back toward the barn. "You shouldn't be out in this."

"Help me. Clint, I need you. Please." She swiped at her eyes, and it was clear rain wasn't the reason her cheeks were wet. "It blew over, and Bumpo is trapped underneath it." Her shoulders bounced as she cried.

Sloshing through the mud, I braced my shoulder against the shelter and shoved. It had taken two of us to get this into place. Moving it by myself would be no easy task. The mud made it nearly impossible.

Repeated attempts ended with my feet sliding out from under me.

With Bones barking his suggestion that we go back inside, I braced a boot against the nearest fence post and inhaled, mustering every bit of muscle strength. With a shove, I managed to get the shelter lifted a few inches. "Hurry. But don't get under it."

Joji dropped to her stomach and pulled Bumpo out. "He's out!"

The grateful goat bleated, then ran for the barn. At least he had a bit of sense. Bones followed Bumpo.

As I helped Joji out of the mud, lightning splintered the sky. Thunder roared a half second later. I picked her up, crushing her to my chest, and ran into the barn.

After putting her down on the milking stool, I hugged her. "You cannot be out in this weather. Are you okay?"

"Says the guy who just drove over here. How did you know where to find me?"

I scanned her, checking for injuries. "Any sane person would be inside, so I checked the barn."

She flashed a weak smile, then her eyes filled with tears. "I'm so glad you came. I herded the goats into the barn after the winds picked up, but that thing blew over, and I couldn't get to Bumpo." She rested her head on my chest. "Thank you for coming to check on the goats."

A flash of lightning raised the hairs on my arms. And the electricity in the air had my brain jumbled. I rubbed at a spot of mud on her cheek. "I'm not here because of the goats."

Her gaze snapped to mine. And the look in her eyes shoved reason into a dark corner.

"You came for me?"

This woman was a magnet, and I was a pile of metal shavings.

Silencing alarm bells that were screaming for me to walk away, I nodded and trailed a finger along her jawline.

A crack of thunder sounded the moment my lips brushed against hers.

Slowly, her hand slid around my neck, and I tightened my embrace.

Bones whined, but I ignored him.

"Mr. Clint, I'm scared." Mason stood in the barn with my rain poncho wrapped around him.

Words wouldn't connect into sentences. And panic gripped me. "How—"

Joji patted my chest, then clutched my arm as she stepped off the milking stool. "Hey there, Mason."

He nodded. "You are the nice bread lady."

"That's me. Why don't we all go inside and figure out how you ended up here while we enjoy a cup of hot chocolate?" She glanced back at me. "Ask his dad if he can have that."

His dad! Kent was probably worried sick. And Parker.

I slid my phone out of my pocket and winced at the ten missed calls. I clicked on Kent's name and didn't wait long for him to answer. "Mason's with me. He must've climbed into my truck, but I didn't see him. We're at Joji's."

"Okay. Is he all right?" Kent's voice trembled. "I shouldn't have left him."

"He's fine. Just a bit scared of the storm. Nothing a mug of hot chocolate won't fix. Is it okay if he has a cup?"

"Yes. Yeah. That's fine." Relief was evident in Kent's every word. "You going to stay there until after the storm passes?"

"Yes. I'll text when I'm headed back." After ending the call, I tucked my phone away. "Want me to carry you?"

Mason bobbed his head up and down.

We made sure the barn was secure and that Bumpo was safely with his cohorts, then trudged back to the house. On the porch, I kicked off my muddy boots and pointed at the trailer. "Is Cami here?"

Joji shook her head. "Had a date tonight. Won't be home until later." She laughed as she glanced at the front of her shirt and jeans. "I'm a mess. Once I get you guys hot chocolate, I'm going to change clothes. I'll wait on the shower."

"Good choice. I never shower during a lightning storm." I picked up a rag off the counter and tossed it to Mason. "We're all a mess. Little buddy, you can use this to wipe your face. Sorry I got mud on your shirt."

He shrugged. "Daddy doesn't care if I get muddy."

"You have a good dad." I gave up trying to wipe the mud off my shirt.

Mason grinned as Joji set butter and toast in front of him. "Mr. Clint, did you have a good daddy?"

I could feel Joji staring at me. "Miss Joji makes the best toast because she makes the best bread. And I hope you like cats. She has lots of them."

"Lately, they've spent almost as much time wandering outside as they have inside. But tonight, they are all inside." Joji poured hot water into two mugs. "Marshmallows?"

Mason nodded. "Lots of them."

"Same for me." I leaned back in the chair, watching her buzz about. "How'd you end up with me?"

He stared at the table. "Don't be mad."

"I'm not mad. Not at all."

"I just got into a truck. Then the lightning crashed, and I hid."

I could've continued asking questions, but the answers wouldn't change anything. "Well, you're safe now, and your daddy knows where you are."

This happy little scene twisted my gut into knots. It was

good that kiss had been interrupted. I should never have let my feelings stomp out reason. Our friendship was good. Why risk that?

I just had to figure out how to make sure she was on the same page.

CHAPTER 25

JOJI

I knew the moment Clint pulled away that our moment of bliss was gone forever. Whatever battle raged inside him resumed.

But I'd learned something. A kiss didn't break the curse. I was beginning to think only he could do that.

The good thing was, no matter what happened, I had the memory of that kiss. The bad thing was, I had the memory of that kiss. And inconveniently it popped up when I needed it filed away.

And gathered in the house while the storm raged outside did little to quell the memory. Every flash of lightning yanked my thoughts back to the moment when his lips touched mine.

Hail crashed against the windows. This storm didn't sound like it was letting up any time soon.

After changing into clean clothes, I walked back out to the kitchen with a laundry basket on my hip. "Once you finish the hot chocolate, should we watch a movie?"

Mason grinned. "Yes! And this storm isn't so scary."

Clint glanced out the window, and I didn't think he held the same sentiment.

He downed the last of his hot cocoa. "Movie sounds good, but I can't sit on your couch with this shirt on."

"Give it to me. I'll wash it with my muddy clothes."

He scrubbed at his whiskers, looked down at his shirt, then nodded. As I expected, he had an undershirt on underneath. "I'll just keep this on. It's not as bad."

Mason undid the snaps on his little cowboy shirt. "You can wash mine too."

I dropped both shirts in the basket. "Y'all choose the movie. I'll be out in a jiff."

Watching the way Mason looked up to Clint and mimicked him made my heart race. It was sweet. And Clint deserved to be a role model.

Once the washer was going, I stepped out of the laundry room but froze when I heard my name.

"Is Miss Joji your girlfriend?" Mason asked the question I wanted the answer to.

Clint delayed responding for a few heartbeats. "She's my friend. I was worried about her because of the storm."

"Daddy hugs me when he's worried. And sometimes he kisses my head. But not on the lips."

"Good advice, kid." Clint sounded just as tormented as the night he lugged Boingo out of the bed of my truck.

I took a cleansing breath. Dealing with my emotions could wait until later. "What did y'all decide on?"

Clint sprang up out of his chair. "Oh, hi. I haven't even looked." He picked up the dishes off the table. "Let me help you get this cleaned up."

Mason tried to hide a yawn.

"I think someone is sleepy. Maybe you should choose something calming that will relax him."

"I'll find something." Clint set the mugs in the sink before walking into the living room.

He turned on a documentary about building planes. "How's this? You like planes?"

Mason crawled up onto the sofa. "Cool!"

That little boy was asleep before I finished cleaning up in the kitchen.

He was curled up on one end of the couch with his feet shoved up against Clint's leg.

Clint tapped the empty cushion on the other side of him. "There's room. And I can change this if you want to watch something else."

"Whatever." I sat down beside Clint. "Sounds quieter outside."

He showed me his phone. "Yeah, but we have another round headed our way. This one shouldn't be as bad. But I texted Kent, letting him know we'd be here a bit longer."

"You were great with Mason. He looks up to you."

He shrugged. "I feel for the kid, but Kent is doing a really good job."

Knowing what Clint needed to hear, I forced words out of my mouth. "I think maybe what happened in the barn was a mistake."

After a sharp intake, he nodded. "Me too. I mean . . . I was so worried, and . . ."

I rubbed his arm. "I know."

His shoulders relaxed. "I appreciate you saying something. If I were wanting romance, you'd be on my list, but I—"

"You have a list?"

He gave a nervous chuckle. "No. I guess one person doesn't count as a list."

"I'm teasing you."

"Gathered that." He chewed his lip, staring at the television. "My dislike of redheads had nothing to do with why Scarlett left me. She was a handful. Temperamental. Hard to please. I assumed all redheads were the same, which sounds really stupid when I say it out loud. But all redheads reminded me of Scarlett, and I can't think about her without thinking about why she left."

I bit back all the awful things I wanted to say about a woman I'd never met. "Why'd she leave?"

Clint shook his head. "Cute kid, isn't he?"

I took the cue and let the conversation jump to a different topic. "He's adorable. But I can't say that when he's awake. I doubt he'd think that was a compliment."

"Did you want kids?"

"Once upon a time I did. But that wasn't part of my plan, I guess. And I have no regrets. It took me a long while to get to the point where I could say that honestly." Maybe I should've had my fingers crossed because I did regret telling Clint that our kiss was a mistake.

"The day I helped you out of the tree, you said there hadn't been a Mr. Sparks. How is that possible?" He lifted his eyebrows, hesitation flickering in his eyes. Asking personal questions had him pushing out of his comfort zone.

"I lost my fiancé when I was young. After that, I avoided serious relationships for a long time. By the time I thought I was ready, I'd been red tagged and moved to the clearance shelf."

Staring at me, he blinked. "Clearance shelf?"

"I was considered old."

He shook his head. "I'm sorry about your fiancé. That must've been horrible."

"It was. But I've learned not to live life thinking about what could've been."

It was quiet as Clint rubbed at a spot of mud on his jeans. "Scarlett wanted kids."

I sat silent. If I opened my mouth now, sobs would pour out.

"We dated through most of high school. I hadn't exactly seen a healthy relationship modeled, except Beau's parents, but apparently, I'm dense. Anyway, after high school, I married her. For years we tried to have kids. I went to appointments with her and agreed to testing. It was awful."

"I'm sorry."

"Even now when I close my eyes, I can picture the moment the doctor gave us the news that I was the problem. Scarlett didn't speak to me all the way home."

Anger made my face warm.

"When we got back to the house, she packed a bag. As she walked out the door, she told me to box up her stuff and that she'd send someone to pick it up." He sighed. "That's why she left."

"You deserved better."

"I'm not sad that she left. She took her drama with her. But . . ." He shook his head.

"I don't know what she said to you that you aren't telling me, but she was wrong." I tried to keep my redheaded temper in check.

"She didn't say anything but the truth. I wasn't man enough to give her what she wanted."

"Goat dookie." I said it too loud, and Mason stirred.

Any woman who thought Clint wasn't man enough lacked coherent thought. Other words might have described her better, but there was a kid present.

Clint laughed and patted the kid's leg. "That's why we're friends. You know exactly what to say." His brow pinched and his smile fell away. "Please don't say anything. No one else knows what I've told you. Not even Ava or Beau."

"I won't say a word to anyone." I crossed my arms to keep myself from touching him. "Tell me about your parents."

"Might as well toss all my dirty laundry out for you to see."

"Hold that thought. Let me throw the clothes in the dryer." I raced back to the laundry room, needing the break to shed my tears. Once the dryer was going, I wiped my face and resumed my friendly smile. "Go ahead."

"My dad was a drunk, the mean and abusive kind. He never laid a hand on me or Ava. All his anger was focused on my mother. But he stopped hitting on her when he noticed I was big enough to fight back." Clint rolled his head from side to side. "I never fought him, but I remember the night he came in plastered and shouting. I was the only one awake. Wouldn't have mattered anyway because I slept on the couch, so I always knew when he came home. My mother had gone to sleep in Ava's room. She did that when she knew he'd be coming home drunk. Dad yelled and shouted for her." Clint scrubbed his face. "I stood up and told him she was asleep. And he looked up at me. I wasn't a whole lot taller, but enough. And I saw fear."

I swallowed and gave up trying to keep my hands to myself. I wrapped both of my hands around his. "I bet she was grateful."

"Not so sure about that. He moved out the next day. We barely scraped by after he left."

I used his undershirt to wipe my eyes. "I'm not sure about this movie. It's making me cry."

He smiled but didn't laugh. "It wasn't all bad. I had Beau as a friend. And I loved his parents. They helped me quite a bit during my high school years. In fact, his dad gave me the money to buy my truck. And I made payments to him every week. After he died, Beau handed me an envelope with my name on it. His dad had saved all that money to give it back to me." Clint draped an arm around me. "But now you get why I can't."

He said it as such fact I didn't have the heart to argue, but I didn't get it. Not in the least.

Mason sat up, rubbing his eyes. "I have to go to the bathroom."

Clint checked his phone. "We should probably go. It looks like the storm has moved on."

I glanced back toward the laundry room. "Those shirts aren't dry yet."

Mason danced. "Where's the bathroom?"

"Sorry, it's that door right there." I pointed. "Don't step on Bones. He likes to sleep by that door."

Mason petted the dog and every cat in sight before closing himself into the bathroom.

"We'll get the shirts later." Clint kissed my head. "Thanks for listening."

And thanks to the conversation with Mason, I knew what that kiss on the head meant.

Friends.

TWO DAYS LATER, I stepped up to Clint's door with his clean shirt in one hand and a freshly baked loaf of bread in the other. I tucked the shirt under my arm and knocked.

He pulled open the door. "Hey, come in."

"I can't stay. I need to drop Mason's shirt at his house." I motioned uphill as if Clint didn't know where Mason lived.

Clint leaned on the doorframe. "Did the storm do any damage?"

"Not that I've noticed. Thanks for getting that shelter upright. I must've missed y'all."

"Cami said you were on your biweekly café visit."

"It's not exactly a café in Paris, but I like it." I stepped backward.

"Did the buyer come by for those goats?"

"He did. They are gone. And not surprisingly, he didn't want to know their names. Thanks again for fixing the shelter." I turned and ran down the stairs.

I wanted to be friends with Clint, but the constant desire to throw myself into his arms made it a tad harder to do the friends thing.

He stayed at the door until I pulled away.

I'd run off too quickly, but that was the best I could do right now.

When I knocked on Kent's door, the curtains moved, and Mason's face appeared in the window. He waved, then disappeared. A second later, the door swung open.

"Hi, Miss Joji! Daddy is taking a shower."

"My timing is impeccable, isn't it?"

He cocked his head. "What's that mean? Is that like kissing on the lips?"

"No. Nothing like that at all."

Asking a four-year-old to keep a secret was a bad idea. But deep inside I hoped word wouldn't spread about the kiss in the barn.

I held out the shirt. "Just wanted to drop this off for you."

"Thanks. That's my favorite shirt. Miss Ava bought it for me."

"And I brought you bread."

"Yum! I'll have toast for dinner."

"I'll see you later." I hurried off the porch before Kent's shower got interrupted. I didn't need more stories following me around.

When I arrived home, I found a note taped to my door. *Come to the trailer.*

I really wasn't in the mood to drag goats back to their pen, but that's what I'd signed on for by buying a goat farm apparently.

But maybe goats weren't the reason for the invitation. There was a familiar car parked in front of the trailer. Cami had company. Haley was here.

I knocked, then pushed open the door when Cami hollered for me to come in.

"Surprise!" Haley, Nacha, and Cami screamed as I walked inside.

Streamers hung all around the room, and a cake sat on the coffee table.

"My birthday isn't for another three weeks."

Haley laughed. "We know, but if we'd waited, you wouldn't have been surprised. Zach, Harper, and Hank will be here soon. They said not to cut the cake until they arrived."

"Y'all didn't have to do all this." I hugged each of them.

"We're glad you're living here." Nacha patted the couch. "Now sit and tell us all about your cowboy before the guys get here."

"Nothing to tell. We're friends." I had to repeat that truth to others as often as I had to say it to myself.

No one seemed convinced.

Cami rolled her eyes. "He's totally into her. Totally." She dramatically rested a hand on her heart. "Coming to check on her because she didn't answer his messages about closing up the chicken coop."

"You eavesdropped?" I'd nearly forgotten Cami was there that night.

"Uh, yeah. It was like a scene out of one of those old people romance movies." She laughed. "Not old, but you know what I mean."

"You mean old."

Haley handed me a box. "This is from us. You can open it now. You don't have to wait on the guys."

Fear nibbled on my insides. "Should I be worried?"

"It doesn't bite," Nacha said.

I tore away the paper. "Good. Because around here, I have plenty of things that do."

Inside the box was a tiny castle.

Haley cleared her throat and rubbed the pendant on her necklace. "That's a little reminder that it's never too late to live your own fairy tale."

These three would never know how much this silly resin castle meant to me and how much it hurt.

"Thank you. And I assure you, if my prince arrives, I won't send him packing. But I might make him milk the goats."

CHAPTER 26

*J*oji hadn't called or messaged in a week, which wasn't completely unusual, but it had me nervous. She'd been different after I told her my story.

I should've kept my mouth shut.

Thinking about Joji while my head was buried in the tractor engine inhibited my ability to work quickly. The phone buzzing in my back pocket didn't help either. I bumped my head on the hood as I yanked out the phone, checking to see if it was Joji.

"Important call?" Beau wore a smug grin.

I swiped to dismiss the call before sticking the phone back in my pocket. "Didn't recognize the number. Thought it might be one of the guys."

"They have *my* number." He held up his phone.

"True." I went back to work and ignored my phone when it buzzed again and again. That was one determined telemarketer.

When it started buzzing for the fourth time, I wiped

grease off my fingers and answered the number I didn't recognize. "Hello?"

"Clint, it's Cami."

Why was Cami calling so incessantly?

I turned away from Beau and walked out of the shop. "What's wrong? Is Joji okay?" Fishing in my pocket for keys, I headed for my truck. "Where are you? I'm on my way."

"Whoa, cowboy. You have a thing about assuming the worst, don't you? Joji's fine. I'm not sure how my hello was confused with a call for help, but whatever."

"You didn't say hello." I shoved the keys back in my pocket. "And you called me over and over."

She laughed. "Oops. Sorry. Hello, Clint. How are you?"

"Want do you want, Cami?" I didn't have the time or patience for games.

"The back door of the barn is making that *eeeek eeeek* sound again."

Why was she calling to tell me about a squeaky door on Joji's farm? But asking her why meant I'd get a thirty-minute explanation, and I didn't have the desire to listen to that.

"I can run by later and oil the hinges." I mentally added it to my list for the day.

"Today?"

"Yes. I'll be by there later today."

Why was she being so persistent about a squeaky door? The goats didn't care.

"Good, but don't come between seven and eight because Joji will be doing that goat yoga class, and you'll probably want to talk to her. I'm guessing."

"Tell Joji I'll be by to fix it."

"Thanks, Clint. You're the best. Well, I like Harper better, but you know what I mean."

"Is that all you need?" I stayed outside the shop, trying to wrap up the conversation out of Beau's earshot.

"Yep. Bye." She ended the call with the same enthusiasm she'd used in her greeting.

Beau stuck his head outside. "Is Joji okay?"

"She's fine." I went back to work on the tractor.

"If you need to go over there . . ."

I stood up, taking extra care not to bang my head. "I don't. Let's get back to work."

Beau laughed. "Whatever you say."

After another few minutes, the tractor rumbled to life.

He flashed a thumbs up. "That didn't take you long."

"Good thing. I have a long list today." Before he could ask any other questions, I headed out. "Call me if you need anything."

"Will do."

Beau drove the tractor out of the shop as I drove away.

I'd managed to get out of there without too many questions. My relationship with Joji, friendship or otherwise, was nobody else's business.

I drove out and met Dallas in the north pasture. Thankfully, he never asked questions about my personal life.

Some days on the ranch were hard. Other days were hard and long.

At dinnertime, I hadn't yet finished up everything that needed to be done. But no matter what, I'd make it over to Joji's to deal with the squeaky barn door.

Why hadn't Joji called me herself?

After a break for dinner, I wrapped up the last few things on my list, then I went to Joji's. About half past seven, I parked outside her barn. Showing up in the middle of the lesson probably disappointed Cami, but she'd live.

And me? I'd get to see Joji in her little leggings. That was always a treat.

Joji grinned and waved as I strode into the barn. Even

from far away, I could see that she was surprised. Cami must not have mentioned that I was coming.

I oiled the hinges, then opened and closed the door to make sure it didn't make a sound.

Satisfied Cami couldn't make it eek anymore, I checked the time. There were less than ten minutes left in the yoga class, so I decided to wait. Leaving without talking to Joji would seem rude. Besides, I wanted to know that things were okay.

I dragged the stool toward the wall, then took a seat, pulling my hat down over my face and tilting my head back against the wall. No harm in closing my eyes while I waited.

Not surprisingly, I dozed off.

A little while later, Joji lifted my hat. "Did you come to see me or are you hiding from someone?"

I scrubbed my face. "I stopped by to fix the creaky door but figured I'd at least say howdy before heading home."

Her brow pinched, and she tilted her head. "How did . . ." She spun around and looked at the door. "It only started making noise after the storm."

I shrugged. Until I figured out what Cami was up to, I saw no point in concerning Joji.

"No matter. Thank you." She rubbed my arm, a habit I was beginning to like a bit too much.

"Anytime." I covered a yawn.

"Thanks for staying long enough to say hi. But you need sleep. Will you make it home all right?"

"I'll be fine."

She walked with me to my truck. "Text me when you get to your porch. I'd say when you get home, but you'll probably fall asleep as soon as you walk in the door."

"Most likely. But I'll shoot you a message."

It was easy to keep that promise because I thought about Joji all the way home. When I parked outside the cabin, I shot off a text before getting out of my truck. *Made it home. Goodnight.*

Her response was one hundred percent Joji. *Sweet dreams.*

TWO DAYS LATER, I dropped the bags of dog food and cat food into the bed of my truck, then went back inside to get the rest of my stuff. Once everything was loaded into the bed, I climbed into the truck.

Before I backed out of the parking space, my phone rang. I answered, recognizing the number. "Hello, Cami."

"Hiya! I just wanted to let you know that one of the bulbs on Joji's porch is burned out."

"A lightbulb?"

"Yeah, surely it doesn't take more than one cowboy to change a lightbulb."

"Very funny. Anything else?"

She was quiet a second. "Not that I've been able to find."

What was that supposed to mean? Then it dawned on me.

I could be dense, but even I could see what Cami was doing. "I'll take care of the light." A thought sparked before I hung up. "Cami."

"Yeah?"

"Where's a good place to get coffee in Stadtburg?"

My question was hopefully vague enough that she wouldn't know why I asked. I wasn't even sure what motivated the question. Not true. Seeing Joji motivated me.

"In the strip mall across from that good barbeque place. Doughnuts and coffee and lunch stuff. Super yummy."

"Thanks."

"Clint, wait," Cami shouted. "You should wait until eleven."

"Is that when the place makes fresh coffee?"

"Something like that. Bye." She ended the call.

I had an hour to kill before my café visit, so after running back inside to buy lightbulbs, I drove to the specialty store and picked up the items Ava had requested. What did she plan to do with rose water?

A few minutes after eleven, I pulled into the parking lot and spotted Joji's car. I parked next to her classic Mustang, then wandered into the doughnut shop.

"Good morning. What can I get you?" A pretty brunette flashed a smile.

I scanned the menu on the wall. "I'll take two ham-and-cheese kolaches and a lemon-filled doughnut. Oh, and a coffee." It took every ounce of will-power not to turn around and scan the small dining area.

"Coming right up." The woman buzzed around, then handed me a plate and a cup of coffee. "Napkins, sugar, and all that good stuff are right over there."

I looked where she pointed, but my gaze settled on the table next to the coffee station. "Thanks."

Joji smiled and tapped the chair next to her. "I didn't expect to see you in here."

"I'm on my way back from a store run. Coffee sounded good." I dropped into the chair. "You come in here often?"

"At least twice a week. You caught me on my biweekly visit. I like being around people."

"That's where we're different." I noticed the half-eaten ham-and-cheese kolache on her plate. "But we like the same foods it seems."

She laughed. "More than you know. I ate my lemon-filled doughnut first."

Why didn't it surprise me that she enjoyed dessert first?

"Tell me about your café in Paris."

She sighed, but not in sad way. "I rented a tiny little apartment in Paris, and right down the street was this picturesque café. I went there all the time. My favorite table was outside, near the corner of the building. I could see people on two different streets from there." She closed her eyes and smiled as if she were back there again. "I'd order macarons, these little colorful cookies with some sort of frosting or something inside. Oh, I miss those."

"Where else did you visit?"

Every question I asked garnered me stories and smiles. And long after my lunch and doughnut were gone, I listened as she related stories from her travels.

"I've rambled on way too long. You have a ranch to run." She patted my arm.

"I should go, but this was fun." I picked up my hat.

Joji cleaned up the table. "I'll walk out with you."

Things were back to normal, and I was happy. My horror stories hadn't chased her off. Joji was still my friend.

She turned toward the counter as I pushed open the door. "Bye, Tessa!"

I tipped my hat, then followed Joji outside.

"Ignore the faces plastered to the window of the photography studio next door." Joji shook her head. "They're embarrassing."

I glanced back, and Cami waved before giving me a thumbs up. She'd gotten the wrong idea.

I couldn't do anything right.

JUST BEFORE DINNER, I drove over to Joji's. I had just enough time to replace the lightbulb before heading to the dining hall.

Carrying the lightbulbs, I walked onto the porch. Bones lifted his head, then promptly put it back down, his tail wagging.

"Happy to see me?" I checked to be sure I'd grabbed the right wattage.

As I reached up to unscrew the bulb, the door opened. "I am happy to see you, but you shouldn't do that when the light is on."

"Then will you turn it off?"

She flipped the switch. "Not that I'm complaining, but why are you on my porch replacing a lightbulb?"

I screwed in the new bulb. "Someone mentioned that your porch light was out. Turn it on to make sure it's working."

When she turned it on, light cascaded over the porch.

"You're all set."

Joji pulled the door open the rest of the way. "Oh. Well, thanks for fixing it. Want to come in?"

"Ava is making fried chicken. It's good. You should join us." While I wanted to spend time with Joji, spending time together with others around seemed like the friendly thing to do.

"Sounds good. Let me grab my keys."

"I don't mind if you ride with me. I can drive you back."

"Perfect." Joji patted Bones on the head. "I'm leaving you in charge. Make sure everyone behaves."

I loved how she talked to both animals and people with the same vivacious authenticity.

In comparison, I seemed like a walled-off grump. Maybe I was.

CHAPTER 27

JOJI

*S*tanding at the window, I looked out and watched Cami near the chicken coop. She scanned the enclosure, then walked around to each fence post and tried to wiggle it. What was that girl doing? For the last three days, she'd been scouting the farm as if she were trying to find problems.

The fourth fence post moved a bit, which seemingly made her quite happy.

Grinning from ear to ear, she tapped away on her phone. Was she the reason Clint had shown up to change my light-bulb last week?

I liked Cami, but I didn't understand her. Why was she trying to find things that needed fixing? I'm sure somehow in her brain it made perfect sense.

She put her earbuds in, then danced her way to the goat pens.

Was she going to check all the posts in there too?

I didn't have time to monitor her craziness. I had cheese to make.

Living dangerously, I'd signed up for a table at the farmers' market this weekend. And if I planned to sell cheese, I had to make cheese.

With music blaring, I set to work. Eventually, I'd teach Cami to help, but not today. I wanted the alone time.

After mixing the acid into the milk and heating it, I danced around the kitchen. With the bowls and lids all set out, I waited for the liquid to drain off.

Tomorrow, I'd be doing this all over again. I'd probably end up skipping my café visit.

Leaning on the counter, I stared at the little castle sitting in my kitchen window. "When he walked into the doughnut shop, my heart stopped. I so enjoy talking to him. And it's obvious that he likes talking to me. At least I think so. Am I crazy for wishing things will change?"

I was having a deep and heartfelt conversation with a toy castle. Was that so weird? I checked the timer. Waiting was the hardest part of making cheese.

Doing nothing made me crazy, so I mixed dough while the whey dripped through the cheesecloth. It would be good to have some bread made in case Clint stopped by.

But he had no reason to stop by.

That all changed a minute later when a shipping notification popped up in my email. My new milking contraption was on its way.

I shot off a quick text to Clint. *Milking system will be here in a week! I'm so excited.*

He'd already built the platform and had multiple milking stations just waiting for the new equipment. His response made me smile. *What day? I'll put it on my calendar.*

I gave him the information, then sent one more text: *See you then!*

He replied right away. *I'll be by before then. There's a wobbly post in the chicken coop I want to take a look at.*

Cami?

Yep. Did you put her in charge of maintenance? He followed his text with a laughing emoji.

You don't have to take care of that. I'm sorry she's bothering you. I felt horrible that Cami was expecting him to fix stuff on the farm.

I don't mind, but I might not make it by today. This was a typical response from Clint. He was such a great guy and always willing to help even when he was busy.

No hurry. And thank you. I tossed the phone aside and went back to my cheesemaking.

Singing along to the music, I filled my containers. On a roll, I mixed the next batch of cheese, determined to get it all finished today. I could probably wrap this all up before it was time for evening chores. And then I could still enjoy watching people tomorrow.

The hours passed, and satisfaction put a smile on my face. I'd been extra productive today. After tucking the last of the cheese in the fridge and pulling the bread out of the oven, I danced a circle in the kitchen with my arms in the air and my eyes closed.

I enjoyed music more when my eyes were closed. The notes penetrated my soul.

The song ended, and I inhaled, waiting for the next one to start.

"It's not a wonder you weigh nothing." Clint was standing just inside the door.

"Clint! You startled me." I turned down the music, then pulled out the cutting board and bread knife. "You smelled the bread from all the way over on the ranch?"

He laughed as he hung his hat on the hook. "That's just a nice surprise. And, for the record, I knocked. Twice."

"How did you know I was decent?"

Grinning, he pointed at the windows. "The curtains are all wide open."

"So much for dancing like no one is watching."

He did that thing where whatever thoughts were making his eyes sparkle did not come out of his mouth.

"Have a seat. Let me grab the butter." I needed better emotional armor if he was going to keep showing up like this. "Bones, you aren't much of a watchdog."

"He knows me. No reason to alert you. I'm not dangerous."

He had no idea how wrong he was. No idea at all.

I set a plate in front of him. "What can I get you to drink?"

"Just water. And that post in the chicken coop barely moves. I wouldn't have called it a wiggle."

"Then don't worry about it. If it weren't so obvious that Cami is nuts for Harper, I'd wonder if she had a crush on you."

Clint choked on his bread.

I tapped his back. "She doesn't. And no offense, but I'm pretty sure she thinks you're old."

"I know why."

"Why is that?" I couldn't wait to hear his answer.

"Because we are old."

I shook my head. "Speak for yourself. But, seriously, I can't figure out why she told you. Is she the one who mentioned the lightbulb?"

He nodded as he ate.

"Why is she telling you about all the stuff wrong on *my* farm?" I slathered butter on a slice of bread. "That makes me sound ungrateful, and you know there's no way I could've done this without you."

"Don't discount yourself. And who knows why Cami does anything? She's more complicated than you are."

"I'm not sure if that's a compliment or not."

He shrugged. "Just a fact."

Once his bread was gone, he stood and stretched. "Wish I

could stay, but I still have a couple things to take care of before dinner."

"Thanks for checking the chicken coop. I'll say something to Cami so that she doesn't keep messaging you."

"Don't worry about it." He put his hat on, tipping it as he walked out the door.

I glanced at the castle. "I wonder if wishing on stars still works at my age."

TYLER WAVED as he hauled bags of compost to the garden. How that man could carry so much on his shoulder was beyond me. Little by little during every yoga class, my plot of weeds had been transformed into what promised to be a great garden in the spring.

And besides having the area all prepped, I got to watch people fall in love. And that was always fun to see. After each yoga class, Jasmine would wander over to see the progress on the garden. That was always her excuse.

Love might be an overstatement. I wasn't sure if Tyler had worked up the nerve to ask her out. But she'd given him lots of opportunities.

Some of these cowboys were complicated.

Ava kicked me. "You going to do yoga or daydream?"

"I was thinking." I shifted into the pose everyone else was doing.

When another truck rumbled up, I dropped onto my mat. Who else was here?

Clint backed his truck up by the garden.

"Now you're daydreaming." Ava giggled.

"Shh." Acting like I was paying attention to Jasmine, I stole glances at Clint.

What was he doing here? Had Cami texted him again?

"He spends a lot of time over here." Lilith nudged Ava.

They were as bad as schoolgirls.

"Pay attention. We'll talk later." I didn't want to be rude to Jasmine, and I didn't want to be distracted.

Clint unloaded posts and bags of something.

How was I supposed to concentrate on finding my inner peace when Clint was over there lifting heavy stuff out of the bed of his pickup?

Boingo climbed onto my back, which only reminded me of climbing that tree thinking I'd save him. My brain jumped from there to Clint helping me out of the tree.

I envied those bags in his arms.

When class ended, I ran over, leaving my mat on the ground. I stopped before I reached the garden and ran back. Those goats would gleefully eat my mat if I left it too long.

With it rolled up and under my arm, I walked over to the garden.

Clint dragged his sleeve across his forehead. "Hey there."

"What's all this?"

"You're all excited about growing vegetables, but you know who else likes vegetables?" He leaned on the contraption in his hand and lifted his eyebrows.

"Goats! I hadn't even thought about that."

"Exactly. And someone happened to mention you had a birthday coming up. This is my gift." He nodded toward the pile of posts. "I'm building you a fence that Boingo can't jump over."

I dropped my mat and threw my arms around him. "You're the best."

The contraption hit the ground, and he lifted me off my feet.

I hung on too long for anyone other than Clint to assume it was just a friendly hug. But because of his lens, that was all he was willing to see.

He set me on my feet. "It might not be done before your birthday, but I'll be out here as often as I can."

"Thank you." I hopped up onto the tailgate of his truck. "What's that thing you were holding?"

"A post-hole digger. Two holes down. Lots to go." He wiped his brow, bringing attention to the sweat beading there.

"I'll be right back out with unsweet tea." I slid down, picked up my mat, and ran inside.

My plan to be quick was derailed when I saw Ava and Lilith sitting at the table.

"Make yourselves at home." I laughed as I grabbed two glasses. "Let me run tea out to the guys, then I'll be back."

"Oh, we'll wait. We have lots of questions." Lilith grinned.

They wouldn't like the answers. I hurried back outside, trying not to spill tea as I walked.

"Here you go." I held out a glass to each of the guys.

Clint downed his in just a few gulps. "Thanks."

Tyler laughed. "I wonder if he even tasted it."

"Just let me know if you need more." I pointed back toward the house. "Ava and Lilith are waiting on me."

"Have fun." Clint drove the post-hole digger into the ground.

I walked back inside, preparing to answer questions that I hated the answers to. "All right, ladies, what do you need?"

Lilith tapped a manicured nail on the table. "We saw that hug. That wasn't a friend hug or a pretend hug. I know from experience. What's going on?"

Ava didn't look up, and I guessed that she knew her brother pretty well.

I poured myself a glass of tea and added heaps of sugar.

Lilith waved her hand. "Hang on. My first question is if you like sweet tea—which the white layer at the bottom of your glass kind of gives that away—why do you have a pitcher of unsweet tea in your fridge?"

"Clint likes unsweet tea." Ava glanced up, and there was something akin to pity in her eyes.

I didn't want that.

"I can't exactly pull the sugar out for people who don't like it. I just add it to my own. And Clint and I are friends. That's all."

Lilith looked from me to Ava, then back to me. "Y'all have talked about it?"

"We have." My nod ended that line of questioning.

"What kind of cake do you want?" Ava knew the perfect time to bring up cake.

"Anything covered in frosting. And if it has a layer of frosting in the middle, that's even better."

Lilith glanced down at her phone. "Gotta go. Beau and I are going out tonight. And I can't go like this." She motioned toward her tight little exercise outfit.

Ava laughed. "I'm thinking he wouldn't mind."

"I mind." She lifted her eyebrows, looking at Ava. "You riding with me?"

"Yeah. Be out in a second." Ava waited until Lilith was outside and all the way to her car. "He cares about you, Joji, but he carries around a lot of baggage. We both do. Mine is mostly layered here on my hips. But give him time. Maybe something will wake him up."

I smiled, not wanting to tip my hand that I knew all about his baggage. "Thanks, Ava." Inching up on my toes, I wrapped her in a hug. "And I'm sorry."

She shrugged. "Life goes on."

Ava was right. The sun would come up tomorrow just like it had yesterday and today.

CHAPTER 28

I downed the rest of my coffee and set the mug next to my plate. "Thanks, Ava. Breakfast was great." If I played my cards right, I could make it to the farmers' market around lunchtime and still have time to work on Joji's fence before dinner.

At the rate I was going, I might have her gift finished in time for her birthday.

Ava snapped her fingers. "Are you even listening?"

"Sorry, what?" I never meant to ignore people when I was thinking.

"I wanted to do something special for Joji's birthday in addition to the cake. Any ideas?" She picked up my plate.

"I'm sure she'll like whatever you make. Sugar is one of her favorite things." I strolled toward the door, then stopped. "Actually, I do have an idea. She talked about some little cookies she had in Paris. Maca-somethings."

"Macarons! I better go find a recipe. Thank you!" Ava rubbed her hands together, her brain already working. "I knew you'd know."

I nodded and hurried out to the truck.

Kent cut me off as I rounded the corner. "Have a second?"

"Sure." I glanced around for Mason. "Where's the little guy?"

"Mason is with Parker. They're going to straighten up the tack room." Kent shoved his hands in his pockets. "Anyway, I wanted to talk to you when I didn't have little ears around. Mason told me all about what happened at the barn. Delicately, I explained to him that he didn't need to talk about it with other people. I can't promise it won't come up. But he hasn't mentioned it since."

"I appreciate that." Saying anything more would only dig a hole for myself. "He's a great kid, and you are doing a super job as a dad. I don't say that lightly."

"Thank you, sir. That's a real compliment." Kent narrowed his eyes. "I will add, that when Mason goes to school, if he starts kissing his friends, I'm coming to find you."

"Fair enough." I shook his hand. "I need to run."

"Same here. I'll catch you later."

Beau walked around from the other side of my truck. "What was that all about?"

"Nothing to worry about."

He shook his head. "What's up with the secrets? As I recall you were the one who warned me about secrets."

"It's need-to-know, not a secret." I grabbed the door handle. "Need anything?"

"To know." He flashed a mischievous grin. "Are you going to check on that tank with the leak?"

"That's where I'm headed." I didn't have time in my plan for small talk.

He climbed into the passenger's side. "I'll ride with you."

"Suit yourself."

He was quiet as we drove. Not unusual for Beau. When

we stopped next to the tank, he rolled his neck from side to side. "How's the fence coming?"

"It's coming. After I finish up a few things here on the ranch, I'll head into town for a bit. Later, I should have time to work on it."

"Is there yoga today?"

I shook my head and scanned the tank. "There isn't but maybe three inches of water in this thing. Hole is probably big." I continued circling the stock tank. "I've seen Lilith out at that class a few times."

Beau grinned. "I really need to get over there one of these days."

"You can help with the fence."

"Maybe."

"Found the hole. Good thing we checked before moving the cows to this pasture." I yanked my boot out of the mud. "Help me get this emptied and loaded. I'll haul it to the shop barn and fix it there."

Beau helped, and once we had it loaded, he checked his phone. "I'll fix it. And while you're at the farmers' market, will you grab some flowers?"

"Flowers? Don't you think it's a little weird for me to be buying your wife flowers?" I turned the truck around and headed toward the barn.

"Yes, but they aren't for Lilith. Well, she told me to get some, but they're for Joji."

"Her birthday isn't for another four days."

He shrugged. "I just follow orders."

"I guess I can get flowers." How was I supposed to get flowers, then help Joji without her seeing the flowers? "I'll try. I planned to help Joji. She's selling cheese today. And I'm guessing the flowers are a surprise. Not sure how I'll be able to hide them."

"I think Lilith just wanted you to give them to Joji today. For the table. To make it look pretty."

Without bothering to keep the edge out of my voice, I said, "I don't need help. And giving her flowers would make her think—"

"What everyone thinks. Clint, you're crazy about her."

Denying it would be lying. "She knows how I feel."

Beau's jaw dropped open. "And you haven't mentioned it? Lilith and Ava will be excited, and they might let me enjoy a quiet evening without asking me if you've said anything to me about Joji."

"She knows I want to be her friend."

He scrubbed his face. "Whatever Scarlett said to you was a long time ago. It's time to move on."

"It has nothing to do with Scarlett." I wanted only the best for Joji, and this broken cowboy didn't come close to making the cut.

We hauled the tank into the barn.

"Thanks for fixing it. I'm headed to the market."

Beau scrunched up his nose. "You should change before you go."

I glanced down at my shirt and jeans. "What a mess."

"I've seen less mud in a mud pie."

Without even giving him a courtesy laugh, I hurried to the truck. "Be back later."

If I hurried, I could make it there in time to help Joji set up the table.

At the cabin, after I'd put on clean clothes, I grabbed a tall mug out of the cabinet. It was big enough to hold flowers if she needed something pretty for the table.

I just wouldn't mention it to Beau or Lilith.

～

I SPOTTED Joji's truck as I drove past the park where the market was held once a month. That woman was trying to wrestle a large cooler out of the bed. I was afraid to ask how she'd gotten it into the truck.

After pulling into the nearest empty spot, I ran across the street toward her. "Let me help you."

A signature Joji smile lit up her face. "This is a fun surprise."

"It's your big day. I wanted to come by. And I plan to get some cheese because now I love it on toast." I lifted the cooler out of the bed. "Lead the way."

"Let me grab this other bin. It isn't heavy." She rested a small plastic tub on her hip. "Getting those extra goats really helped. It takes more time to milk them, but more milk is good."

"People will love the cheese. And that machine will help once it's installed."

"I hope so. Because then Joji's farm will be a business instead of a very expensive hobby." She set the bin on a table. "You can put the cooler back there. I need to get the table-cloth on here." Scanning the other tables, her shoulders slumped. "I should've grabbed something else to put on here. I didn't think about decorating. I was only thinking about cheese. But I brought crackers and a platter so that people could have samples."

"Wait here. I have just the thing." I might not admit to Beau that I'd bought flowers, but it was good I'd grabbed the mug. After grabbing it from my truck, I walked through the market to the flower booth.

An older woman tucked a stray hair into her bun, then smiled. "What ya need, hun?"

"Do you have any blue or purple flowers? Nothing big. It needs to fit in here." I held up the mug.

"How about these?" She picked up a small bouquet with a mix of flowers, most of which were blue and purple.

"Perfect. I'll take it."

She cocked her head. "For someone special?"

"Actually, my friend is—yeah. They're for someone special."

"Give me the mug." She said it in the same tone my first-grade teacher used to ask me to hand over a note being passed—nice but firm.

I handed it over.

She snipped the ends off a few flowers, pulled some greenery from a tub in the back, and fussed with the arrangement before handing it back. "Seven dollars."

I dropped a ten on the table. "Thanks."

"I hope she likes them."

I did too.

Joji was still setting up the table, and people were gathered around, asking questions. Her smile widened when she saw the flowers. "That's just what this table needs."

I let her put it where it looked best. "How can I help?"

Handing me a pair of plastic gloves, she nodded toward the platter. "Will you spread cheese on crackers and put them out for people to taste?"

"On it." My hands were not made for spreading cheese on crackers, but I did my best.

I dropped samples onto the glass plate, then spread more cheese, trying not to break yet another cracker.

"It's a good thing the cheese tastes just as good when the crackers are broken." A man chuckled. "The presentation leaves a lot to be desired."

It seemed funny to see a guy in faded jeans and work boots talking about food presentation.

"I'm all thumbs, but the cheese makes up for it. Have you

tasted it?" I wasn't trying to impress anyone with my presentation, but I wanted today to be a success for Joji.

The guy picked up the only unbroken cracker. "Wow. This is great. I've been looking for a local cheesemaker."

"Oh?"

"I'm the chef at the restaurant that opened at the winery." His gaze swept over Joji, then landed on her empty ring finger.

Maybe it didn't, but that was how it looked to me. I maintained my smile. "The place out on Henry-Miller Road?"

"That's the place." His gaze stayed on Joji.

"Well, she makes it all herself."

He tapped the table. "I'm going to walk around and grab a few other samples, then I'll be back to chat with her when there isn't such a crowd. She's popular today." He strolled away while I tried to figure out how I could make it to market days every month.

Someone had to look out for Joji when wolves were prowling about.

The crowd thinned a few minutes later, and she fanned herself. "It's been so busy."

"Cheese is selling fast. A chef stopped by a bit ago. He tasted it and said he'd be back to talk to you."

She slapped a hand over her heart. "A chef?"

"He looks more like he'd fit in on a ranch. But he said he was at the new place at the winery."

Her eyes widened. "The *Cowboy Chef?*"

"I guess." Clearly, I wasn't in the know.

"I've read about him. Maybe one night, I'll have dinner over there. People rave about the food."

As if summoned by our conversation, the chef sauntered up to the table. "I'm Jeffrey. And your cheese is delicious. Your boyfriend was telling me that you make it all yourself."

I held my breath, wondering how she'd respond to that. I

saw no point in correcting the man, but that was selfish. Maybe he was what she needed to be happy.

Joji picked up a mini log and a small tub. "I do. Take these, and if you're interested in more, call me." She spun around and dug through the plastic tub.

He and I both avoided looking at her backside while she searched. I glared at him, and he stared at the cheese.

Grinning, she held out a business card. "Here's my number."

He dropped it into his shirt pocket. "I'll be in touch."

I had mixed feelings about that.

For two hours while she talked to customers, I kept the platter supplied with broken samples, and the inventory dwindled.

By lunchtime, the cheese was sold out.

Fanning herself, she dropped into a chair. "I can't believe it all sold so quickly. And thank you. I could not have done this without your help."

"Happy to do it."

"Haley offered, but I told her I wouldn't need help. Boy, I sure was wrong."

"She came by. You were talking to that chef."

That chef had come by the table more than once. Interest in cheese was appreciated. Interest in Joji was not.

Joji rubbed my arm. "I'll have to call her later. Let me make you dinner . . . as a thank you."

"I never turn down dinner."

"I'll throw in dessert if you help me load my truck." She winked.

"Deal."

She packed up the few things still sitting out. "You didn't get cheese! I'm sorry."

"Don't worry about it. I know where to find you."

"After milking in the morning, I'll make you some. Wait. I can't tomorrow, but I can on Monday or Tuesday."

"Whenever." I smiled as she sniffed the flowers, making a mental note of how much she seemed to like them.

Friends gave friends flowers, right?

.

CHAPTER 29

A truck rumbled outside, and I ran out the front door, expecting to see Clint getting out of his truck.

Instead, the Cowboy Chef slid out of his truck. "Afternoon. When we spoke earlier today, you said it was okay if I dropped by to see the operation. Is now okay? The gate was open, so I figured you were here."

"Sure. Let me pull my boots on."

Kittens skirted past me and ran down the front steps. Bones sauntered after them as if he'd been designated to keep them out of trouble.

"You've got quite the farm here. What other animals do you have?"

I pulled the door closed as I walked outside. I didn't want Boingo eating my pillows. "Goats, chickens, cats, and a dog. That's it for now."

"Do you sell eggs?" The chef followed behind me as I walked to the barn.

"I don't. Anything I don't use goes to the ranch on the other side of my fence. Good neighbors and all that."

Surprisingly, Bones had given up his babysitting job and was trotting next to me. He almost never did that.

"This is the barn as you can see. This afternoon Clint is setting up the automated milking stations. That will be a huge timesaver." I explained what goats we had and showed him around the pens. "And as short as this tour was, that's really all there is to see, Mr. Carpenter."

"Call me Jeffrey. And I like what I see." He cocked an eyebrow and smiled.

I'd seen that smug look more than once in my lifetime. And it was never appreciated.

"She's got a great set-up here." Clint strolled into the barn, and Bones wagged his tail.

I considered wagging mine, then decided against it.

"Oh, it's you." Jeffrey stuck out his hand. "Good to see you again. I didn't catch your name the other day. I'm Jeffrey Carpenter."

"Clint Jackson." After shaking hands, Clint walked over toward the boxes stacked along the wall. "Don't mind me. I'm going to get her new system assembled."

Jeffrey scanned the barn, probably trying to think of other questions. "I don't want to be in the way. I'm excited about getting more cheese. And if you'd like to dine at my place—I know reservations are hard to get right now—call and tell them Jeffrey said to seat you at his table." He handed me a business card. "Call the number at the bottom. That's reserved for my special guests."

"Thank you." I wasn't sure why I was in a hurry to escort the man out of the barn. "And I'll have another batch of cheese ready next week."

"Perfect." He tipped his hat before walking to his truck.

Before Jeffrey was out of earshot, I turned to Clint. "I made a batch of cheese just for you this morning. It's in the fridge." I waved the business card before stuffing it in my back pocket. "And I have an order for another batch."

"I heard." Clint didn't look up from the parts as he set them on the platform.

After climbing up onto the platform, I sat on the edge and let my feet dangle over the side. "You don't like him, do you?"

"He seems nice. *Very* friendly."

"Friendly is one way to put it. I think he expects all women to swoon over the idea of a man in cowboy boots cooking up a fancy dinner."

Clint glanced up. "Does sort of seem that way."

"Want to know what makes me swoon?" I lay back and rolled onto my side next to the parts he'd lined up.

"What?" Lines crinkled near the corners of his eyes. "Those little cookies you ate in Paris?"

"Well, yes, but I meant the kind of man that makes me swoon."

"Then yes, please tell." He started connecting parts.

"Cowboys who don't cook."

Was that general enough not to make him uncomfortable?

One side of his mouth lifted. "That's a big group. But poor Jeffrey. I'm sure he'd be disappointed to hear that."

I shrugged and shifted to my back. "I have a low tolerance for guys like that."

"Like what?"

"He thought you were my boyfriend, but he still showed up unannounced, doing his sweet talk thing."

"You mean things like 'I like what I see'?" Clint altered his voice and gave a passable impersonation of the chef.

Why couldn't this dream of a man see what a catch he was?

"Exactly like that. I'm glad you showed up when you did. His expression was priceless."

Clint chuckled. "I guess he didn't expect to find me here on the farm."

"Sure didn't seem like it."

"This shouldn't take long to put together. And I should be able to finish the garden fence tomorrow before the festivities. Beau said he'd help me put up the last bit of fencing."

"Festivities? You make it sound like a huge deal. Cake, punch, and music with my friends and family. If we're lucky, the temperature will drop a few degrees."

"That'd be nice."

I slid off the platform. "You don't need me talking your ear off. And I'm not even sure how to thank you anymore. Dinner doesn't seem like a fair exchange."

He smiled. "I'm happy with that deal."

What was the possibility of adding an addendum?

THE FLOWERS in the mug hadn't yet wilted, and I loved having them in my kitchen window next to my little castle. It gave me hope.

After the rain all morning, the sun was a welcome sight. I needed sunlight on my birthday.

My patience with Clint amazed even me. Typically, I would've spewed my feelings—loudly and passionately—but he didn't need anyone else berating him.

Waiting was still hard. Especially since I wasn't sure there was a light at the end of the tunnel or, in my case, another kiss.

That was what I wanted for my birthday. A kiss. Not just for the kiss itself, but for all it would mean. I didn't want us to end the day the same way we started it. Just friends.

But I had no idea how to make that happen. Besides the rain we'd had earlier, the weather was supposed to be clear.

No storms in the forecast. Tapping the top of my castle, I sighed. "If I rub you, do you grant wishes?"

The banging and other noises generated by work on the fence had stopped. I peeked out the window in my bedroom to check the progress. They guys weren't out there. Had they finished already?

Surely, Clint hadn't left without saying goodbye.

I ran out to the front porch. Both trucks were still there, and I looked around for Beau and Clint.

"Up here!" Bare-chested, Clint waved from atop the barn.

I blinked, wishing he were on the ground where I could see him up close and not way up there on the barn. On the barn?

He sat back on his heels. "I noticed the roof was leaking, and . . ."

His words faded to a mumble as panic thumped on the inside of my head. Oscar's face appeared for a second, then faded away. Being on top a barn on my birthday was bad luck. I couldn't lose someone else I loved. I couldn't.

The thumping changed to ringing, and everything went dark.

CHAPTER 30

CLINT

*J*ust as Joji's gaze snapped to me, she went pale, then collapsed. And her head connected with the porch rail on the way down, sending alarm rippling through me. I needed to get to her.

I scrambled to the edge of the roof, but Beau had already left his post to check on her. Trusting that ladder without someone steadying the bottom was a risk I didn't need to be taking right now. Watching, I held my breath as Beau leaned over her.

Was she talking? Conscious? Being so far from her tore at my heart.

"Is she okay?" I tested the ladder to see if it was stable.

Beau gave a nod, but he didn't even turn around.

Screaming at him to hold the ladder would leave Joji unattended. But we needed to get her to a hospital.

"Come hold this ladder! I need to get down. We need to get her medical attention."

Cami burst out of her trailer. "Medical attention? What happened?"

"Joji fainted and hit her head." All my hollering was making my throat raw.

She shook her head and shot me the disappointed teacher look as she knelt next to Joji.

"Get me off this blasted barn!" Any shred of patience I'd had when Beau was the only one here to check on Joji was gone. "Now! Come hold this ladder."

Beau stood but stayed by the porch.

"Get over here!" I was getting hoarse from yelling.

"I'm coming." Beau ran to the base of the ladder. "Got it. As soon as you're down, we'll take her to urgent care. She'll get there faster if we just go."

Lilith's SUV pulled up, and Ava and Lilith jumped out as soon as it stopped rolling. In a second, they were swarmed around Joji.

Ava turned to face me as I ran up. "What happened?"

Cami huffed. "Clint went and climbed up on the barn roof." She rolled her eyes as if I should know why that was such a horrible thing.

Ava slapped a hand to her heart. "Oh no. And on her birthday."

Just as I was about to ask why that was so terrible, Joji opened her eyes. "I'm fine. I don't need to go—" She tried to stand, then dropped back down.

I leaned down and got nose to nose with her. "I'm taking you to get checked out. Please don't argue with me."

Tears pooled in her eyes, and she opened her arms. "I'm glad you didn't die."

The statement made no sense to me, but that wasn't unusual when I was talking with Joji. "You and me both, Trouble." I hugged her close. "Ava, grab her purse. Beau, you drive."

Lilith waved us toward the SUV. "Take mine. It'll be better than your old truck."

Cami wrung her hands. "I'll call Haley and everyone."

Ava shoved my shirt into my hand. "You'll probably need this."

"Thanks." I carried Joji to the SUV, loaded her into the backseat, then buckled her in.

When I slid in beside her, she rested her head on my arm.

"Don't go to sleep. You need to stay awake. And tell me if you start to feel nauseous or if your vision goes blurry." I stared at her eyes, wishing I knew what I was supposed to be looking for to make sure she was okay.

She nodded. "Later, when my head isn't pounding, I'll tell you why I fainted."

"You were so impressed by how I look without a shirt?"

"That's the other reason. But I'll have to look more later."

I brushed her cheek. "I'm sorry it hurts. But keep your eyes open. Look at me."

Her gaze met mine, and she flashed a weak smile. "I made a wish on my castle."

"I hope your wish comes true." I kissed her head. "Just stay awake. Tell me how you make the cheese. Step by step."

More than once her eyelids closed while she told me the steps. And when they closed, I squeezed her hand. "Keep looking at me."

She pulled on my arm, and I leaned down.

"Are you feeling okay?"

"I don't feel so good." She reached up and patted my chest. "We're almost there."

Her eyes slipped closed, and I glanced up to see Beau looking at me in the rearview mirror.

"You don't have to say it. I know." Being stuck on a roof when she was hurt brought on one of those lightbulb moments like the kind in cartoons. I cared about Joji. Deeply.

He grinned. "I think that's our lucky ladder."

Joji opened her eyes, but her hand didn't move. "Stay off the barn."

"I will. I promise. I'll call someone to patch the roof. The storm must've damaged it. We just hadn't noticed."

"Our storm." Her thoughts were plastered on her face in a wide smile.

"Yeah, Trouble. Our storm." I couldn't wait to kiss her again, but first I needed to make sure she was going to be all right.

≈

PACING IN THE WAITING AREA, I glanced at the door every time it opened. Joji had been back with the doctors a while. It felt like a long while, but my perception of time was definitely skewed.

"There are plenty of chairs." Beau rubbed the back of his neck.

I shook my head. "Can't sit. Sorry if my pacing is making you crazy."

"I get it. Hopefully, we'll hear something soon."

"You and me both. How could I have been so dense?" I whirled around and pointed at him. "Don't answer that."

He smiled. "I'm glad you figured things out. Finally."

"I hope I didn't realize it too late."

"I'd offer to go get our lucky ladder, but Ava has probably hidden it again by now. Where'd you find it anyway?"

"I promised her I wouldn't tell you." I took a deep breath, trying to stay calm. "Why is it taking so long?"

A nurse in hot pink scrubs appeared in the doorway. "Is there a Clint out here?"

"That's me." I sprinted to the door.

She smiled. "Miss Sparks requested that you go back there with her."

"Sure. Yeah. Great." I walked next to the nurse, wishing she'd move a little faster.

"Right in here." She knocked on a door.

A faint "Come in" sounded from inside.

The room was dark except for the glow of a computer screen. Joji sat on the padded bench. And it was obvious she wasn't feeling well because she was still.

"Hey there." I hurried over and wrapped her in a hug.

With a sigh, she snuggled against me. "The doctor said it didn't seem too bad. Only a mild concussion. But I don't want to be by myself."

"I'm here." I reined in my hopes.

Right now, Joji needed a friend.

After a knock, a man in a white coat entered the room. Using my keen intellect, I surmised that he was the doctor.

Keeping one arm around Joji, I extended my hand. "She's gonna be okay?"

He nodded. "She needs to take it easy for a couple of days. Brain rest. Here's a sheet that explains what she can and can't do. And she needs someone to stay with her for the first twenty-four to forty-eight hours. Will that be a problem?"

"Not at all." I considered it my personal mission to make sure she wasn't left alone.

I absorbed every instruction the doctor offered as Joji relaxed against me. "Hey, wake up. You shouldn't sleep yet." I flashed back to high school when I'd had my concussion.

The doctor shook his head. "You don't need to keep her awake. She can sleep. The sheet covers all that. Any other questions?"

"Can we go?"

"Yes. Just check out at the front desk." He walked out of the room.

I brushed my hand on Joji's cheek. "Are you okay to walk?"

"I'm fine. Just hold my hand." She tangled her fingers with mine. "Thank you. You're a good friend."

My hope disintegrated. Friend. I'd chosen that, but now I wanted something different.

"Let's get you home."

WITH JOJI CURLED up on her sofa next to me, using my leg as a pillow, I watched her chest rise and fall. When she stirred, I patted her hip, then she'd snuggle closer.

I liked when she did that.

It seemed weird letting her sleep. Years ago, they'd made us stay awake for hours. Playing football, I'd had my fair share of bang ups.

But the doctor assured us it was fine for her to sleep as long as someone was with her.

I volunteered.

Hank and Haley made me promise to update them every hour. I just added them to the list. Cami had already texted eight times. And Ava was probably baking a slew of pies. She baked when she worried.

Joji mumbled, but I couldn't make out anything she said. The doctor called it a mild concussion, which gave me hope that in a few days, Joji would feel like herself again.

Right now, only one of us was getting a brain rest. Mine was churning thoughts so quickly, it almost made me tired. But I wouldn't let myself sleep for a while yet.

Watching her breathe in and out, I tried to figure out what I wanted to say to her once she was feeling better.

My phone buzzed, signaling me that it was time to wake her. I'd read the instruction sheet twice and was following instructions to the letter. Someone (me) needed to wake her up regularly. And as much as I hated interrupting her sleep, making sure she was okay was more important.

"Hey, Joji. Wake up for me." I brushed red curls out of her face.

Her eyes fluttered open. "You're here."

"I am."

She pushed up to a sitting position. "You don't have to stay. I'm fine here by myself. Cami isn't far away, and—"

"To quote a wise person I know—*goat dookie*. You think I'm letting Cami take care of you? That girl can't tell a billy from a nanny. Besides, the doctor said someone had to be with you *all the time* for the first twenty-four hours." I brushed a thumb along her cheek. "You're stuck with me."

Her gaze locked to mine, and she swallowed.

"I'll be here until you're feeling better." I wrapped my hand around hers. "Right here."

My walls had come down, but that conversation could wait until she felt better. Right now, she just needed to know that no matter what, I'd take care of her.

She glanced down at her hand in mine. "I remember him saying I couldn't do a bunch of stuff."

"He did. You need to let your brain rest."

Without pulling her hand away, she leaned her head on my arm. "Thank you."

I shifted and put my arm around her, tucking her against my side. "Want anything? Food? Something to drink?"

"Clint."

Threading my fingers through her hair, I kissed the top of her head. "Yes?"

"That's my answer." She looked up at me. "You've been beating yourself up because you couldn't give Scarlett what she wanted. And she was completely wrong about you not being man enough."

"Joji, we don't need to talk about—"

She pressed a finger to my lips.

It was a nice way of shutting me up.

"You can give me what *I* want." She gazed at me a second, then buried her face in my shirt.

I pulled her closer. "What do you want, Joji?" At the moment, I would agree to give her almost anything.

"You."

Praying I wouldn't complicate her recovery, I shifted her into my lap and caught her lips with mine. Soft and gentle, my kiss was meant to show her how I felt without over-whelming her brain. But if hers was anything like mine, it was spinning like a leaf caught in dust devil.

I broke away long before I wanted to.

She rested her head on my chest. "Take me to the hospital."

"What? What's wrong?" I pulled her away from my chest and scanned her face. "Is your vision blurry?"

"I'm think I'm hallucinating. Or did you really just kiss me?"

I hugged her to me. "Don't scare me like that. Once you've recovered, I'll kiss you every day."

"Twice."

"Deal."

She closed her eyes. "When it's time for me to wake up again, wake me with a kiss. And maybe with your shirt off."

"All right, Sleeping Beauty. I will." Holding her, I sent a text update one handed. *Joji woke up without any issues. We talked for a bit, and now she's sleeping again.*

A flurry of *Thanks for the update* messages popped up on my phone, but the text from Ava stood out. *Did you tell her?*

I stared at the woman asleep in my lap. She made me feel like a prince. No one else had ever made me feel that way.

Not yet, but she knows. I hit send on my answer, then set the phone aside, giving Joji my full attention.

This whirlwind of a woman had stormed into my heart, mending pieces I thought would never go back together.

Now I had to wait until she was mended to elaborate on my feelings.

CHAPTER 31

JOJI

I woke up in my own bed with no memory of climbing under the covers. I had vague memories of being kissed during the night. Or had that been a dream?

The blinds were all closed, but the sun wasn't yet up anyway. Carefully rolling out of bed, I tried to piece together how and when I'd changed clothes. I didn't have my unicorn pajamas on when I'd walked out onto the porch.

But thinking hurt.

Maybe coffee would help.

Making it to the kitchen seemed like an achievable goal.

Bones jumped down off the foot of my bed, his tail wagging.

"Hey, boy. Did you watch over me last night?"

He kept pace next to me as I made my way down the hall.

Ava smiled as I walked up to the counter. "Morning. How are you feeling?"

Why was Ava here?

Had kissing Clint and being snuggled in his arms been only a dream? A long vivid dream. The doctor had mentioned possible confusion, but the kisses had seemed so real.

"I've been better." I dropped into a chair. "Will you make me coffee?"

She waggled her finger. "No. No coffee until you are better. The caffeine isn't good when you have a concussion."

Resigned to a day without coffee, I nodded. "Okay."

She set a plate in front of me. "Eggs and toast."

"Do you know if Cami took care of the morning chores?" I asked about the chores, hoping I'd learn more about where Clint was . . . or if he'd even been here at all.

Ava propped her hand on her hips. "You don't need to be thinking about any of that. We're taking care of it."

"Yesterday is fuzzy. I was in jeans when I walked out to the porch. How did I . . ." Trying a different angle might get me an answer to my unasked question about whether Clint had been here with me last night.

Ava sat down and folded her hands. "When you got back here after seeing the doctor, I helped you change clothes. You wouldn't have been comfortable in jeans." The woman was maddeningly unhelpful.

"Thanks for the food." Breakfast tasted good. Probably because I hadn't eaten since lunch the day before.

I had a vivid recollection of Clint offering me food, but I'd only wanted to sleep.

Boots sounded on the steps, and I dropped my fork.

"That man has no idea how loud he is. I'll tell him to step more quietly." Ava hurried toward the door.

"No. Leave him alone." I stood and waited next to the table.

He pushed open the door, gently closed it behind him, then reached up to hang his hat on the hook. "Have you checked on her?"

Ava pointed at me.

Clint turned, and his eyes widened. "You're up." He stepped closer but stopped before he made it to the table. The hesitation in his pinched brow made me wish I could remember more clearly.

He inched closer. "How are you feeling?"

"Confused." I glanced at Ava, then back to Clint before turning to look at the sofa. "I thought . . ."

A smile spread across his face as he raced toward me. "I was here. I promised, remember? But I needed to take care of the animals, so I asked Ava to come make you breakfast."

I leaned into his embrace as he wrapped his arms around me.

He kissed the top of my head, and I questioned my interpretation of that repeated gesture.

Ava tapped my shoulder. "Hug him later. You need to eat." She turned to Clint. "So do you. Sit."

After helping me into my chair, Clint sat down beside me. When Ava turned around and walked to the stove, he brushed his lips on mine.

I grabbed a handful of his shirt, keeping him close. Thinking wasn't required to enjoy this.

Ava cleared her throat, and Clint pulled away.

"Let the woman eat." She shook her head. "Do either of you need anything else? If not, I'm headed back to the ranch to feed the boys."

"We're good." Clint grinned. "And thank you."

She patted his back. "Call if you need me." Stopping after one step, she whirled around. "I let the ranch hands eat your cake. I'll make another once the party is rescheduled. But these"—she tapped a box on the counter—"are for you. I hope you like them." With a wave, Ava slipped out the door.

"What's in the box?"

Laughing, Clint moved the box to the table. "I mentioned that you liked those cookies you had in Paris, so Ava made some." He lifted the lid, revealing a colorful array of macarons.

I grabbed one. "Dessert first."

"Great idea." Clint grinned at me all through breakfast.

Once we'd eaten, he cleaned up our dishes while I sat on the couch doing nothing. Well, I was eating more macarons.

"This is going to be boring." I couldn't even read the sheet to see what I wasn't supposed to do.

He chuckled. "Let your brain rest at least two days. Please." After drying his hands, he walked to the couch and sat down.

I scooted into his lap. "I guess talking is the only way to entertain myself."

"Talk away." He toyed with a curl.

I didn't even want to think about how awful my hair looked. But I loved that Clint looked at me like it didn't matter.

"I can only talk for a bit, then I'll probably close my eyes for a little while."

"Whatever you need to do."

What I needed to do was explain my over-the-top reaction to seeing him on the barn. But how could I do that without saying more than he was ready to hear? Considering that focus and intense thought were on the list of banned activities, I said the first words that popped in my head. "My fiancé Oscar fell off a barn on my birthday and died."

Clint groaned. "Joji, I'm so sorry. I—"

I shut him up with my one-finger trick. "When you hugged me after getting off the roof, I wanted you to hold me forever and never let me go. And I haven't wanted that from anyone in an awfully long time."

He brushed his calloused thumb on my cheek. "We want the same thing. But no more thinking right now. Let your brain rest."

I sealed my lips to his. No thinking required.

TWO DAYS LATER, I woke up feeling more like myself. When the front door closed, I slid out of bed and yanked on my boots. A surprise attack was the only way I was getting past Ava and out of the house.

I made it all the way to the front door and had my hand on the knob when Clint laughed.

"Tired of me already?"

"I thought you were out there doing chores." I walked up to him, anticipating another kiss.

"Nope." He lifted me onto the counter. "Finished those an hour ago. I was out there drinking coffee. Since you can't have any, I didn't want the house to smell like freshly brewed coffee. Cami gave me a cup. It's not as good as yours, but it's better than nothing." He rested his hands on my hips. "Seems like you're feeling better."

"Tons better." I trailed a finger through his whiskers. "You haven't shaved in days."

"I had other things on my mind."

"Me." I pulled him to my lips.

He broke away sooner than I expected. "Now that you're feeling better, there are things I want to say."

"And I want to hear, but I need food. This woman cannot live on kisses alone." I slipped off the counter and pulled out what I needed to make my favorite cheese toast. "Who went to the store?"

"I sent Cami with a list. And don't tell her I said this, but she's not so bad." He leaned back against the counter. "You sure you're okay to cook?"

"Fine. I hardly have to think about making this. Muscle memory." Any time I walked past him, I inched up to steal a kiss. Then I brewed a pot of the coffee I knew he loved. "I won't drink it, but I miss the aroma."

He watched me buzz around the kitchen and leaned down for a kiss anytime I came close to him. "When I was on that barn and you went down, panic slapped sense into me. The way I'd been acting wasn't fair to you. My feelings were clear to everyone, but you let me continue in the charade that we were only friends."

I bumped my hand against his. "I let you stay in your cocoon. I wanted to believe you'd break out of it when you were ready. But when I saw you on the barn, I was afraid I'd lose you too."

"The first time I met you, you had my heart racing and my mind reeling."

I handed him a mug of coffee. "That's because you were terrified of my hair."

"And when I helped you out of that tree and you pulled my hat off. . ." He closed his eyes and shook his head. "After that, I couldn't get you out of my head."

Shoving aside the last remnants of fear, I asked the question I needed to know the answer to. "Where do we go from here?"

"I figured you'd need a few days to recover, and I didn't want to rush that." He set his mug down. "I made us a dinner reservation for Friday night. We'll be seated at the chef's private table."

"You called Jeffrey?"

"His assistant answered. And I only mentioned that you and a guest were reserving a table. He might be surprised to see me." Clint took my hand. "I guess what I'm trying to say is, I want to build a relationship with you. Do they call it dating at our age?"

"They can call it anything they want. I'm completely on board." I loved him, but just like I'd waited for him before, I'd wait again until he was ready for those words.

For such a big guy, relationship-wise he took baby steps.

He kissed my forehead. "After our toast, feel up to a little bit of daylight?"

"Yes! I'm craving the sun. And I miss my goats and chickens. And the cats." I patted Bones as he walked up beside me on cue. "This guy kept close to me. I bet he's ready to be outside."

"Besides going out when necessary, that dog would *not* leave your side. The first night, we argued about who got the floor next to your bed." Clint scratched the dog behind the ears. "I won. Sort of. I got the floor, but he jumped up and slept at the foot of the bed. I didn't fit at the foot of the bed." He winked.

That kind of talk would cause thinking.

"I should probably call Haley to let her know I'm okay."

"I've been keeping them posted. But when you feel up to it, I know she'd love to talk to you. And I promised Cami she could pop in and say a hello when you felt better."

"Tell her to head on over. I'll make a few more slices of toast." I turned, but Clint didn't let go of me.

"For the record, I love your hair."

He was using the L word much sooner than I'd expected. It was about my hair, but I still counted that as progress.

"What about my goats?"

He crushed me against him and lifted me off my feet. "Even your goats."

Then he kissed me like he had in the barn. A kiss full of passion, electricity, and unspoken promises.

The door creaked, but he didn't break away.

Whoever it was could wait.

Cami cleared her throat. "Well, this is embarrassing."

Clint pulled back and tweaked my nose. "Only for you, Cami."

Clint and Cami were going to drive each other crazy, and I'd enjoy watching them.

CHAPTER 32

I adjusted my tie as I walked onto the porch, trying to ignore the feeling of being choked. Not nervous about spending time with Joji, I was nervous about dining in a fancy restaurant. At least the place allowed jeans. But the coat and tie were required. Wearing that should show her how much I care.

After a deep breath, I knocked on Joji's door.

She pulled it open and left me speechless. Wearing a blue fitted dress that showed off her legs, she turned in a circle. "You like?"

I held out the bouquet of wildflowers I'd picked before coming over. "I love."

Beckoning me inside, she dumped shriveled flowers out of my mug and tucked in the new bouquet. "When I was getting ready, I realized you haven't seen me in a dress. And you look amazing."

I drank in the sight of her, feeling like the luckiest man alive. "You're beautiful, Joji. Every inch of you."

A blush crept up her cheeks.

"And if Jeffrey says so, I'm going to knock him out cold."

Her eyes widened, and she laughed. "Probably better that you don't. If he comes to the table, I'll just have to distract you."

"That's a plan I can live with." I held out my arm. "Should we take your truck?"

"Are you kidding? I can't sit next to you in mine. We're taking yours."

In the truck, she patted my leg, then left her hand resting there. "I've been looking forward to this all week. I know we see each other every day, but . . ." She shrugged.

"Leaving the ranch makes it feel more official?" Keeping my eyes on the road required focus when what I wanted to do was stare at her.

"I think so."

"I'm counting on you to help me. You've traveled the world. I've hardly left the state. Knowing which fork to use isn't something I learned ranching."

"Whatever help you need, darlin'."

I needed her. More than that, I wanted her.

We parked outside the restaurant, and after getting out, I held out my arm to her. Smiling, she slid her hand down my arm and slipped her small hand in mine.

Because of our special reservation, the hostess treated us like we were VIPs.

She led us to a table in the corner. "Your server will be with you shortly."

And she was right. A guy in black slacks and a starched white shirt smiled as he approached the table. "The chef will be out in a few minutes, but while you wait, what can I get you to drink?"

I nodded to Joji.

"Sweet tea for me." She patted my leg.

"Water and black coffee."

The server didn't even have one of those little notepads to write down the order. "I'll have those right out."

Whatever my opinion of Jeffrey, his restaurant was nice.

After drinks arrived, Jeffrey strolled up to the table. He didn't look happy to see me, but that was to be expected.

Joji beamed as he described the night's specials. But the whole time, her hand was wrapped in mine.

She asked how he liked the cheese and talked to him about the different offerings. When he mentioned an amuse-bouche, I stopped listening. They were speaking a language I didn't understand.

I'd eat whatever Joji suggested . . . as long as steak showed up in front of me at some point.

Jeffrey smiled at Joji, acting almost as if I wasn't even there.

Joji squeezed my hand. "It all sounds delicious. Thank you."

"Thanks for coming in tonight. I hope you *both* have a wonderful evening." Jeffrey nodded and motioned as if he was tipping an invisible hat.

"Thanks." I could be a gracious winner. Besides, it wasn't as if I'd won her in battle.

All through dinner, Joji and I talked. Conversation flowed as naturally as it did when we were standing in the barn. She was the same vivacious person no matter where she was.

Amazingly, I made it through dinner without making any major faux pas. And as she set her fork down after finishing dessert, I took her hand. "Joji, I've already told you how you took up permanent residence in my head. But besides feeling like I didn't deserve you, I thought we were too different."

"Opposites?"

"Look at us. Even from far away, people can see how

different we are, but"—I tapped the lapel over my heart —"they can't see in here. They can't see the way my heart flip-flops when you come near me or the way your touch soothes me when I'm letting thoughts chew on my brain. They can't see how much I love you . . . red hair and all."

Tears pooled in her eyes. "I love you too, Clint."

Nodding, I kissed her hand. "Now, as soon as I pay this bill, let's go because I have a surprise."

"Another surprise?" Candlelight reflected in her eyes, intensifying the look of excitement.

"I've seen how you react to surprises. You love them."

Her smile widened. "You know me well."

I paid the tab, then escorted her out of the restaurant. With a little help from our friends and family, the surprise was ready and waiting.

We turned into the farm, and she leaned forward in her seat. The barn was all lit up, and music danced in the air.

I put the truck in park. "Happy birthday. They rescheduled your party. We'll have to eat dessert twice."

She hugged me. "I could just about live on kisses and dessert."

"One more thing." I pointed into the goat pen closest to where we were parked. "Those two are going to need names."

She slapped a hand over her mouth, then scrambled to get out of the truck.

Laughing, I followed her to the fence.

"Llamas!" She pulled my arms around her. "Rescues?"

"No, I contacted someone who was selling them. Because you aren't like most people." And for that I'd be eternally grateful. "They're a birthday gift."

"You already built me the fence." She turned to face me, then inched up on her toes. "I've been on my own almost thirty years. I don't *need* anyone. But just so you don't think it was my concussion talking, I'll say it again. I *want* you. *You* make me happy." After a quick kiss, she tugged me toward the barn. "Let's go party. We have lots of reasons to celebrate."

Thanks to Joji, I was much more aware of all those reasons. "We sure do."

CHAPTER 33

JOJI

*C*lint and I had spent the summer getting to know each other. In the autumn months, we fell more in love.

We made it a point to have dinner together every night, sometimes at the ranch, sometimes at my place. And on the mornings when Cami wasn't taking care of things, I tackled chores a little earlier, then rushed over to the ranch to have breakfast. Taking him coffee was my excuse, but we both knew it was just so I could see him more than once a day.

I didn't want him shirking his ranch duties. He loved ranching, and I could get up a little earlier to support that.

Carrying a thermos full of coffee, I stepped into the dining hall. When I did, silence fell over the room.

Clint jumped up and gave me a quick kiss. "Morning, gorgeous."

"Hi." I handed him the thermos before dropping into the chair next to his. "Good morning, everyone."

A plate of pancakes appeared in front me thanks to Ava.

Dallas passed the syrup down the table. "You seem sunnier than normal this morning."

"I love this weather, and there is a yoga class tonight. I have three goat mamas who will be delivering any day now. All around, life is good."

"Sounds like lots of reasons to smile." He cut into his pancakes, then shot a glance at Tyler.

Tyler broke a piece of bacon in half. "I'll be out tonight to install the drip lines in the garden."

"Thanks, Tyler." I tried not to giggle when Clint poked me in the side.

We all knew why Tyler spent so much time in the garden, but I didn't have the heart to tease him about it.

Parker rose from the table and carried his empty plate to the big sink. "Thanks, Ava. I'll be in the barn if anyone needs me."

"See you in a bit. Get Trooper ready for me, will you?" Grayson loaded more bacon onto his plate.

"Sure thing." Parker started whistling as soon as he cleared the doorway.

These guys were a happy bunch today.

One by one, the ranch hands left. When Beau and Lilith headed inside, Ava followed them, leaving me alone with Clint.

"I should get back. You have work to do." I rubbed his arm. "Big plans today?"

He nodded as he sipped the last of his coffee. "The guys are helping me with a project." After sitting his mug on the table, he kissed the tip of my nose. "But I'll see you tonight. I'll come to your place. We can order out if you want."

"Or go pick up barbeque."

"Whatever makes you happy." He stood and held out his hand. "I'll walk you to the truck before I go. Unless you want to visit with Ava."

"I need to run. A day of cheesemaking awaits."

He kissed me again, but this time it wasn't on the nose. "See you later."

"Love you." I patted his chest before climbing into my truck.

If someone had whispered in my ear the morning Clint rescued me from the tree, saying that this was where our path would lead, I would've laughed. He still didn't talk excessively. He hadn't shrunk. But he made no attempt to hide his feelings for me.

I'd snagged a real prize.

IT WAS A PERFECT NOVEMBER EVENING. I turned on the outside lights for the yoga session, then tugged my sleeves down. It was just cool enough to need them.

With music playing on my portable speaker, I moved the smaller goats into the area where we held the class. Bumpo was never invited.

But that goat hadn't charged anyone since he'd been pulled out from under the toppled shelter. I still didn't trust him enough to let him attend the sessions.

Sitting on an overturned bucket, I surveyed the farm. My farm. My goal had been to put down roots, and I'd accomplished that in more ways than one. In early spring, I would put down literal roots when I planted my garden.

Jasmine's car pulled into view, and I waved as I walked toward her.

Grinning, she climbed out of the car. "We're going out again tomorrow night!"

"I'm excited for you and Tyler. He put a lot of effort into meeting you." I couldn't complain.

"I know." She sighed. "He's just so . . . amazing."

"Didn't your mama warn you about cowboys?"

She laughed. "You're one to talk!"

I glanced at the time. "I wonder if anyone else is coming. People are usually getting here by now."

"Probably just running late." She set up her mat. "Are things still going well for you and *your* cowboy?"

"Absolutely no complaints." I kept it short because Jasmine had already heard me go on and on about Clint . . . more than once.

Lilith's SUV pulled up just as the other regulars arrived.

Ava set up her mat next to me. "Lilith and I were thinking maybe we'd have a girls' night this weekend. Whatever day works for you. I'll bake a chocolate fudge cake, and we'll watch something sappy and romantic."

"Count me in. That sounds fun." I shooed at the baby goat who tried to chew on my shirt. "I'll see if Josefina is free."

"Yes. Invite her. The more the merrier." Ava quieted as Jasmine started the class.

Only a few minutes later, multiple trucks pulled up. Why were Clint and the other guys here?

When he climbed out of his truck, I fell over laughing. And I wasn't the only one.

He was wearing a t-shirt and leggings, but over his leggings, he had on cut-off jeans. Ridiculous didn't even begin to describe how he looked.

He strolled up and tipped his hat to Jasmine. "Sorry I'm late." After tossing his mat on the ground, he winked at me.

Beau waved a cowbell, and beside him, the ranch hands lined up at the fence, eager to watch the show.

"Where did you get a yoga mat and those pants?" There was no way I was going to be able to concentrate.

"A friend." He put his finger to his lips, then pointed toward the front.

"What are you doing here?"

He shook his head, then pointed at the front again.

Stealing glances at him when I could, I attempted to complete the class. When I folded into a child pose, Jasmine stopped talking. Everyone fell silent. No cowbell. No laughing ranch hands. Even the music stopped.

I picked my head up to see what I was missing.

Clint was on one knee. "Georgia Jean Sparks, you know I love you and that I would do *anything* for you." He pointed to his outfit. "I think this proves that."

I cupped his face with one hand. "You are full of surprises."

"Marry me?" He held out an open box with a simple solitaire nestled in the cushion.

Tears slipping down my cheeks, I kissed him. "Yes." I stuck out my hand. "Put it on me."

He slipped the ring on my finger. "I'm sorry I interrupted your class. I'm going inside your house to get out of this crazy getup. You finish your class, then come find me."

"You know I'm not going to finish this class." I wrapped my arms around his neck, and he carried me toward the house.

Before we walked inside, he kissed my forehead. "You're the best thing that's ever happened to me."

"Of course I am. We were made for each other." I trailed a finger through his beard. "Any chance I can convince you to keep this after November?"

He grinned.

Behind us everyone whooped and hollered.

Clint had managed to surprise me again. And this was the best one yet.

CHAPTER 34

"Give me two minutes to get out of these clothes. Actually, I might need longer than that. I'm not exactly sure how I'm going to get these blasted things off."

"Did you cut up a good pair of jeans?"

"Possibly." I pulled off my t-shirt.

"What do we want to do for dinner?" She turned her hand, watching the light refracting from the ring dance on the walls.

I loved watching her get excited about the smallest of things. And I didn't mean the ring. I meant the light dancing on the walls.

I pulled her hand to my lips. "When I mentioned my plan to propose, Lilith insisted on throwing us an engagement party. I let her because I want to dance with you again. It's tonight."

After grinning at my chest for more than a second, Joji pushed me down the hall. "Hurry up and change, then it's my turn. I can't go like this."

Laughing, I swung the door closed and changed clothes in

record time. When I stepped out of the bedroom, I almost bumped into her.

"How did your clothes get into my bedroom?"

I led her down the hall, then sat down on the sofa, pulling her into my lap. "You were too busy looking at me to see Parker sneaking my stuff inside."

"Was everyone in on it?"

"Yep. And the project the guys were helping me with? Part of them covered ranch duties and the rest of the guys helped me set up for tonight. And Lilith insisted on having it catered."

"It's sweet of her to throw us a party." Joji played with my whiskers. "I really do like your beard."

"Then I'll keep it for a while. And I think Lilith enjoys it."

"Your beard?" Joji lifted her eyebrows in mock accusation.

"Throwing parties. Also, I'm not the least bit disappointed that Mr. Cowboy Chef will be there to help us celebrate."

Joji gaped. "She didn't!"

I winked. "Sure did. And when she hired him to cater it, she told him the reason for the party."

"I'm so excited. About tonight. About everything. We have so much to talk about. When do we want to get married? Should we make a quick run to the courthouse? Where should we live? So many questions."

I kissed her. "These are my answers. That's completely up to you. No. Here. And we can tackle more questions while we dance tonight."

"I think I'm going to request all slow dances tonight."

"Whatever makes you happy." I'd probably be saying that to her often.

By the time she'd changed, everyone had left the farm.

"Who will be there tonight?"

"I made sure everyone knew. Nacha said her mom would be coming and bringing a guest."

Joji beamed. "Mateo. I think they'll be the next to get married. Maybe. Did you invite Cami?"

"She's included in the everyone. I warned her not to spill the beans." I'd worried that Cami would tip off Joji. But not on purpose.

"The girl has hardly been around this week. If she wasn't working, she was at Harper's. Now I know why. She didn't want to mess up the surprise."

"I'll be sure to thank her."

We drove to the venue on the other end of the ranch. Lights were draped across an outdoor dance floor. A band was set up on a stage nearby. And in the smaller gathering space, a long buffet was loaded with food.

Joji grabbed my hand. Delight danced in her eyes. "I got so much more than a farm and a bunch of goats when I bought my place."

"Stuff like that happens at Stargazer Springs Ranch." I was beginning to think it was a place that made dreams come true.

SONG AFTER SONG, Joji and I danced.

When the songs were slow, she peppered me with questions. "If you don't want to go to the courthouse, what do you want?"

I twirled her, then pulled her close to me. "Miss Sparks, you deserve the center aisle, the fancy cake, and the white dress. I want you to have the kind of wedding that little girls dream about. But considering I'm not a girl, you'll have to tell me what that dream looks like."

She leaned her head on my chest. "What about early spring? That would give us a few months to plan. And I know of a great wedding venue."

"Sounds perfect to me."

She brushed red curls out of her face. "Are you really okay living on the goat farm?"

"I'd have to be walled off or lying to say I hate those creatures." I flashed her a smile.

"I'm being serious. We can sell them."

"No, Joji. The past was a long time ago. Now when I see a goat, I think of you." I dipped her, then pulled her close. "I want to marry you, knowing full well that with you I get goats, cats, chickens, llamas, and a dog. And Cami, but I'm not sure how long she'll be hanging around."

"I know. The way Harper looks at her makes me think there might be another wedding being planned soon."

When the song ended, we strolled off the dance floor.

"I'm going to get a bit more to eat. All that dancing has me hungry again." I wiped my brow. "Can I get you anything?"

"No, I'm perfectly happy."

I'd grab her something just in case.

Jeffrey extended his hand as I walked up to the buffet. "I saw you headed this way and wanted to congratulate you. She's quite a catch."

"She is." I turned to watch Joji laughing with Parker and Dag. "And you outdid yourself tonight. The food is amazing."

"Much appreciated." He nodded toward Joji. "What's your secret? Any tips?"

The Cowboy Chef was asking me for advice. What a hoot. He'd get better advice if he asked me how to prepare an amuse-bouche. I hadn't the faintest clue how to make that or how I'd lassoed the right wishing star and ended up with Joji.

I shrugged. "I helped her out of a tree."

He laughed. "Maybe I'll have to try that."

Joji waved me toward the table.

"Nice chatting with you, but my bride-to-be beckons." I carried my plate over and sat down.

She picked up a mini cheese toast round. "Ooh, this looks good. Did you know that I gave him my recipe?"

"I do now." I took a few bites, but then I saw Jeffrey chatting with Ava. "Be right back."

Jeffrey might be a good cook, but he wasn't a good choice for my sister.

I hadn't made it halfway to where they were when Joji grabbed my hand.

She tugged me back toward our table. "They are probably talking about food. Leave them alone. She's not the least bit interested in that self-absorbed cowboy. Trust me."

"How did you—"

She turned and touched her finger to my lips. "Because you are always looking out for the ones you love. And I love that about you."

"I'll never get tired of hearing you say you love me."

She inched up on her toes. "I love you. Let's finish eating, then dance some more."

"As you wish."

EPILOGUE

AVA

Tears wouldn't stop leaking out of my eyes. Seeing my brother in his suit with a grin spread from ear to ear made my heart melt. He'd waited so long for his happily ever after. And I couldn't have picked a better sister-in-law.

Lilith and Beau strolled up the aisle. Then it was my turn. Alone, I marched toward the front, remembering to keep my pace slow. With the tissue clenched in my fist, I dabbed at my eyes, then blinked.

The doors in the back opened, and Mason sauntered up the aisle leading Maude on a leash.

Clint dropped his face into his hand, shaking his head. It seemed like Joji had sprung her own surprise.

Laughter echoed from the guests and increased when Maude tried to eat the pillow out of Mason's hand.

He shook his head. "You can't eat the ring. Then they can't get married."

Clint paled at those words.

Beau shook his head and whispered in Clint's ear, sending a wash of relief over Clint.

When the music changed, he sucked in a breath.

The double doors opened, and Joji stepped in. She lifted the front of her elegant white gown, revealing red boots.

She was definitely the spark (pun intended) Clint needed in his life.

When she made it to the front, she slipped her hand into Clint's and kissed him.

The pastor chuckled, then cleared his throat. "We are gathered here today to celebrate the union of Georgia Jean Sparks and Clint Jackson in matrimony."

He continued talking, and I had trouble focusing. It was easy to pretend the pastor wasn't there when I had my back to him, but it was polite to give attention to the person speaking. But looking at Mad Dog, while not at all a chore, had me thinking about things other than this wedding.

How did a pastor end up with the name Mad Dog? That was a story I wanted to hear. And the way the seams pulled on his suit coat made me wonder about the seams on his shirt. And I also wondered what his arms looked like outside of the shirt or when the shirt was missing altogether.

I wasn't supposed to be thinking about these things during the wedding. Or ever.

The ceremony continued, and when Pastor Mad Dog told Clint he could kiss the bride, Clint lifted Joji off her feet to cheers and whistles.

Pastor Mad Dog closed the little book in his hand. "And now, to all the friends and family who have come to celebrate this marriage, I'd like to present, for the first time anywhere, Mr. & Mrs. Jackson."

Clint swept Joji into his arms, and down the aisle they went.

Beau and Lilith followed, and my palms started to sweat. What had given Joji the grand idea of having Mad Dog escort me out? I'd walked in all by myself. Why couldn't I walk out the same way?

He stepped down off the platform and stood beside me. Looking at the guests, he opened his arms. "I invite you to follow us out and join the happy couple for dinner and dancing." He held out his arm to me.

I rested my hand on his arm, noticing muscles I'm quite sure I wasn't supposed to notice. Or think about.

He led me past the end of the aisle all the way to the reception area. "Clint and Joji look really happy."

"They are." I could answer that without hesitation. "The ceremony was beautiful. You did a great job." Was it polite to compliment the pastor for saying the same things he said at every wedding? At least I hadn't complimented him on his smooth voice. Or the muscles on his arms.

"Thank you. And Ava, you look beautiful today."

Compliments about my looks sent my brain into panic mode. "Save room for dessert. In addition to the wedding cake, I made several pies." Talking about food always steered conversations in a more comfortable direction.

He smiled. "I'm being beckoned, but perhaps later, I'll come find you."

"Sure." I waited until he walked away before dragging my palms down the sides of my dress.

I missed my spot serving food. But I was here to celebrate with Joji and Clint, not to hide behind the counter.

Lilith eased up beside me. "He's a looker, isn't he?"

"Is he? All I see is the pastor. I think it's impolite to comment on how he looks."

"You mean it's impolite to say the pastor is hot?" Thankfully, her voice was at a whisper. "You should talk to him."

He was surrounded by several women who wore smiles so wide plastic surgery might be required to get their faces back to normal. Whatever he was saying had them greatly entertained.

He glanced up and caught me staring.

Embarrassed, I spun around. "I'm not going to talk to him."

"Ava, he seeks you out all the time. I think he wants to talk to you."

I knew better than to assume he was interested in me. "He likes my pies."

"He does, but I'm not sure that's all he likes." She hugged me. "Don't sell yourself short."

It wasn't that I didn't believe in happily ever afters. But life had taught me they were only for other people. And I was okay with that.

Mostly.

I took my seat next to Joji at the head table and squeezed her hand. "Everything is just perfect."

She nodded, her eyes misty with tears. "It is. And I hope you don't mind, but I invited Mad Dog to sit up here with us. I'm not sure I want him sitting with the ranch hands. Because I'm not sure those guys can behave themselves. Or worse, he'd fit right in." She giggled. "That would be funny."

I glanced at the empty chair beside me. "No problem." I plastered on a smile, hoping I wouldn't embarrass myself horribly before the evening ended.

But tonight wasn't about me. We were all here celebrating true love.

I just needed to stop thinking about Mad Dog's arms.

Turn the page for a BONUS epilogue.

BONUS EPILOGUE

CLINT

*J*oji sat cross-legged on the floor, grinning at me as I strummed on the guitar. On cue, she belted out the lyrics.

Given her reaction, was it any wonder I'd played the guitar more since marrying Joji a year ago than I had in the twenty years prior?

Beau was even playing the drums again.

I couldn't take credit for that. After I'd mentioned to Joji that Beau had a natural talent for the drums and that we used to play in a band together, she whispered in Lilith's ear. I had no desire to know how the dots connected after that.

And it was fun playing in the music room. But then one night, Joji nestled into my lap and suggested we bring back the band . . . and play in front of people. I explained that it wasn't possible because we didn't have a bass player.

I didn't know any and felt confident she didn't know any either.

I was wrong.

Who would've guessed that the local preacher was a

talented bass player? Joji apparently. Maybe Ava had mentioned it.

Tonight, the Stargazing Cowboys would make their debut. As much as I loved playing, I couldn't imagine getting on stage for anyone other than my spunky redhead.

She clapped when the song ended. "What time is practice?"

"In an hour." I tucked the guitar into its case, then tugged her into my lap. "Why did I let you talk me into this?"

"You'll be great. It was meant to be. I met this lady at the café who was tasked with putting together a fundraising event for a charity. It's to benefit kids. Anyway, we started talking—that's how I found out what she was working on—and she mentioned how she didn't know where to have it and couldn't find a band. I fixed her up. The event is at Lilith's venue, and y'all are the band."

"So we have you to thank."

Trailing a finger through my closely cropped beard, she whispered in my ear. "You can thank me later. I have a thing for guitar players. Oh!" She sprang out of my lap. "Be right back."

I watched as she ran down the hall, then looked at Bones. "What do you think? Am I going to embarrass myself?"

Bones wagged his tail.

"Thanks for the vote of confidence."

"Ta-da! What do you think?" Joji wore a t-shirt tied at the waist. Across the front was plastered *Stargazing Cowboys*. "I had a few made."

I stood and met her in the middle of the room. "How many?"

"I bought one for you. And the other guys. Of course Lilith wanted one. And I bought one for Ava." She motioned toward the front of her shirt. "The three of us will be sporting these tonight."

"Like groupies."

She walked up to me and rested her hands on my chest. "Exactly like that. I can't wait to hear you play on that stage. I'm really proud of you."

I lifted her onto the counter, trying to figure out how to tell her how much her words meant to me. "Because I play the guitar?"

"Because you are getting on stage tonight to benefit kids when I know that doing so is way outside your comfort zone."

"Thank you. I'm risking it because I've learned that some things outside my comfort zone make life a hundred times better."

A blush crept up her cheeks. "You mean me."

"I do. And I love you. I wish I knew how to explain how much."

"I have an idea." Her eyebrows lifted, and she wrapped her legs around my waist. As she tugged me closer, she whispered, "You should probably let Beau know you'll be a tiny bit late to practice."

I was tapping out an excuse before she finished the last word. "I'm not sure how many times I've used 'tending to the goats' as an excuse. But I'm sure I've used it enough times that he knows not to ask."

"Do you ever think about the day I was in the tree?" Her jumps from one topic to another hardly surprised me anymore.

After tossing the phone onto the counter, I carried her down the hall. "All the time. Mostly I think about getting you out of it."

"That was my favorite part."

I kicked the bedroom door closed with my foot. "You don't say?"

"I was just hanging around waiting for my prince to show up. And you did."

And she'd fallen right into my arms, enchanting me from the very first moment.

Want to read Ava and Mad Dog's story?
Visit RemiCarrington.com for information about
Helped by Ava!

A NOTE TO READERS

Thank you for reading!

When I was writing Beau & Lilith's story (Wrangled by Lilith), I knew Clint would get his own story. And Haley's Aunt Joji was the perfect spark (pun intended) that cowboy needed.

Joji first appeared in the epilogue of *One Guy I'd Never Date* and was a secondary character in *Two Words I'd Never Say Again*. She was such a fun character, and I knew she had to find her own happily ever after.

I had such and enjoyable time writing this story. Now I want a goat and a couple of llamas!

If you loved the story, please consider leaving a review.

Be sure to check out my website for updates about the series and for information about my other books.

www.RemiCarrington.com

ABOUT THE AUTHOR

Remi Carrington is a figment of Pamela Humphrey's imagination. She loves romance & chocolate, enjoys disappearing into a delicious book, and considers people-watching a sport. She was born in the pages of the novel *Just You* and then grew into an alter ego.

She writes sweet romance and romantic comedies set in Texas. Her books are part of the Phrey Press imprint.

facebook.com/remiromance
twitter.com/phreypress
instagram.com/phreypress

Printed in Great Britain
by Amazon

30037575R00151